White Stranger

*Most of the time I forgot I was white . . . that I was the
only white student in St Mark's school . . . Sometimes I'd
catch sight of myself in the cracked mirror and think, who's
that white person? And then realize that* azungu, *that
white stranger, was me.*

Trish longs to be like Grace, already a woman, black
and confident. But Grace treats her like a child, teasing
her—when she isn't ignoring her. Then Grace asks
Trish to visit her home for the Christmas holidays and it
seems as if her dreams of being 'best friends' with Grace
are about to come true at last. But there are painful
discoveries in store for Trish that will shake her new-
found optimism—and there is danger threatening too.
Events build to a climax that will change Trish's life for
ever.

SUSAN GATES was born in Lincolnshire. She has a degree in English
and American Literature from Warwick University. She's worked in
secondary schools in England and in Africa. She now lives in County
Durham and has three children.

WHITE STRANGER

Susan Gates

OXFORD
UNIVERSITY PRESS

OXFORD
UNIVERSITY PRESS

Great Clarendon Street, Oxford OX2 6DP

Oxford University Press is a department of the University of Oxford.
It furthers the University's objective of excellence in research, scholarship,
and education by publishing worldwide in

Oxford New York

Athens Auckland Bangkok Bogotá Buenos Aires Calcutta
Cape Town Chennai Dar es Salaam Delhi Florence Hong Kong Istanbul
Karachi Kuala Lumpur Madrid Melbourne Mexico City Mumbai
Nairobi Paris São Paulo Singapore Taipei Tokyo Toronto Warsaw

and associated companies in Berlin Ibadan

Oxford is a registered trade mark of Oxford University Press
in the UK and in certain other countries

British Library Cataloguing in Publication Data available

ISBN 0 19 271830 4

Typeset by AFS Image Setters Ltd, Glasgow
Printed and bound in Great Britain by Biddles Ltd, www.Biddles.co.uk

PART ONE

ZINJA: AUGUST 1968

ONE

'Don't go in too deep,' I told Grace.

Grace was wading in the water, washing her scarlet and blue *zambia*. The one she looked real fine in.

'There are crocodiles!' I warned her.

'*Cha!*' Gracie threw her head back scornfully. 'There are no crocodiles here. I have never seen one.'

It was the end of August. We were spending the last weekend of the long school vacation by the lake—at the mission house at Zinja. Mum and Dad had let me invite Gracie. I hadn't seen her for nearly three months.

'I haven't seen you since last term,' I protested to Gracie. 'You didn't even answer my letters. You must have some news to tell me. *Something* must have happened in all that time.'

Gracie pouted angrily. 'I told you, girl, nothing happened!' She shrugged: 'Nothing ever happens in my village.'

My other friend, Esther, had come along too. We were getting ready for the dance tonight at the Catholic mission school. Esther had rubbed her face with Ambi skin lightening lotion. Gracie's hair was plaited tight against her head in zigzags. It had taken Esther all morning to do it. I wanted my hair like that. But the plaits wouldn't stay in. So they threaded it with blue glass beads that clicked whenever I moved my head.

Slap, slap, Gracie was whacking her *zambia* on a rock. The lake water foamed pink with Lifebuoy soap.

'You wearing that for the dance tonight?' I asked Gracie.

'I don't know if I going,' said Gracie. 'It will not be

1

much fun, I can tell you. Those Brothers will be everywhere, spying, making sure no one has a nice time.'

She came wading out and spread the *zambia* on a thorn bush to dry.

I felt my face crease up with disappointment. 'I thought you wanted to go—'

'*Eeee,*' said Gracie, 'don't be a cry-baby, Trish. I was lying just now. I will go to the dance. For sure! And I'll wear that *zambia.*'

I had *zambias* too. But I never looked as fine in them as Gracie did. The bright colours made her skin glow. They just made me look pale, washed-out. She knotted them casually round her hips, or under her left armpit. They never fell off. I was always scared my *zambia* would flap open, let all the world see my pimply white thighs.

'Aiee!' Gracie flung herself down on the beach and rolled over onto her belly. 'It is too hot!' She wriggled her hips in the hot sand. 'Trish, maybe tonight you will meet a nice boy,' she teased me.

She had a white bra on with her blue, flouncy school uniform skirt. I was dressed like that too. We got our bras from Mr Khan's shop at the turn-off. He only stocked white ones with thick, white straps—all one size: 36C. I was jealous because, over the long vacation, Gracie had grown a woman's breasts. Now she filled Mr Khan's bras. But I hardly pricked the air inside the cups.

Grace slept in my dormitory at school. She was my best friend, so she was supposed to be on my side. But with Gracie, you could never take that for granted. Sometimes, she teased me, chatted to me, made a big fuss of me. Then seconds later, she'd ignore me, as if I was invisible.

I hated it when Grace paid me no attention. I was fifteen, she was seventeen. She was my hero.

Wow, she had a wicked tongue sometimes—lethal as a boomslang. She made girls and teachers cry. I would have done anything for her, though. I wanted to be like her. I looked up to her like a boy would look up to his gang leader.

I didn't know much about her past—except that she came from some village way out in the bush. She didn't know much about me either. But she wasn't curious. Gracie was self-contained. The lives of other people didn't interest her one bit.

She eased one breast casually out of her bra and inspected it. 'My breasts are sore,' she said. And, casually, put it away again.

That was something else that I envied about her—she was confident, not shy about her body. I wanted to be like that. I wanted her to teach me how. I thought: if I just hang around her, some of her attitude is bound to rub off on me.

'So,' said Gracie, yawning, 'you going to college in UK soon?'

I was thrilled she'd asked me a question—and that she was in a mellow mood. She didn't seem much interested in my answer. Except that she said, 'Gee, I would like to be in your boots.'

I didn't want to talk about UK, even with Gracie. I'd only been twice. And both times I was so small I couldn't remember anything about it. But in a year's time I'd be leaving home to take my A levels at a boarding school there.

Every Christmas we got cards from UK, from aunts and cousins I'd never seen. There were white kids on them, with rosy cheeks, sledging in gloves and scarves. I'd never sledged, never worn gloves, never seen snow. I had no white kids as friends. I was scared. Scared what those white kids in UK would think of me.

Most of the time I forgot I was white, like them. That

3

I was the only white student in St Mark's school. There were no mirrors in our house, only Dad's cracked shaving mirror in the outside chim. Sometimes, cleaning my teeth, I'd catch sight of myself in that cracked mirror and think, 'Who's that white person?' And then realize that *azungu*, that white stranger, was me.

'Put on your hat, Trish,' my mum called out. 'You'll get sunburn.'

My mum was sitting on the *khonde* of the mission house. She had a big floppy white sun hat on. She was reading a book by Jane Austen.

'Put your new hat on,' she mouthed at me, making a halo round her head.

Her voice sounded weary. It almost always sounded like that.

She'd bought me this grass hat from a man weaving hats at the roadside. He was blind, that man, with white upturned eyes, crusty with yellow pus. He had a little boy to lead him around, to be his eyes. And he kept that boy tied by a rope to his leg so he couldn't run away.

I wasn't going to wear any grass hats. It wasn't cool. Gracie never wore sunhats. I ignored my mum.

'*Cha*, that woman, does she never stop nagging?' said Gracie.

'Cissy! Come look at this!' It was Dad, calling to Mum from further up the shore. He was photographing weaver birds' nests in the reeds.

'What does that man want to snap those birds for?' drawled Gracie, curling her lip in disdain.

I didn't like thinking it, especially since Gracie was my hero. But I couldn't help feeling that, sometimes, she didn't give my mum and dad proper respect.

I mean, she was a student at St Mark's school. And they were her teachers. I could sneer at them—that was my special privilege. But I secretly thought Gracie should have been grateful because they had brought her

4

on this weekend away to Zinja. I had begged them to do it. So she should have been grateful to me too, been a bit more friendly, shouldn't she?

But Gracie didn't see things like that—she didn't obey the normal rules of politeness. In fact, she wasn't polite at all. And she wasn't going to be grateful just because it was expected.

My other friend, Esther, was grateful. But Esther was different. Twitchy like a gazelle and timid, Esther was forever saying, 'Thank you,' to my mum. That got on my nerves too.

'Cissy! Come and look!'

Dad came striding along the beach, his leather sandals going flap, flap and his big khaki boy scout shorts flapping too. He had stringy legs with varicose veins like big blue worms crawling under his skin. He had a beard, like Jesus. He taught Science. He was always cheery, full of beans, full of feeble jokes. So uncool it made me cringe. He dashed about everywhere.

Grace had a name for him. She called him *'gudji-gudji'*. Like the spider that hurtled over the concrete floor of our dormitory hut. It had a body flat as a penny on long, racehorse legs. You could empty a can of DOOM trying to kill it. You aimed, squirted, but it was always somewhere else. In the privacy of our dormitory, if she was in a good mood, Grace did a wicked take-off of Dad rushing round the school, busy busy, in his big, flappy shorts. It made us all crease up laughing.

'Cissy!'

My mum gave a long-suffering sigh and put a bookmark in her book.

Mum taught Home Economics—shy, gentle girls like Esther loved her. They flocked round her like doves. Gracie couldn't stand her, of course. Actually, that's not true. The truth is—Gracie hardly noticed my mum existed.

5

Mum came down to the shore in her big, floppy hat to see what Dad was getting so excited about.

I dragged myself up on one elbow. The heat dazed me, made me sleepy as a lizard.

'What's Dad shouting about?'

'It's only the ferry boat,' said Grace. 'What the man making all this fuss for? She come round here every week.'

The ferry boat came steaming through the heat haze, belching black smoke into a perfect blue African sky.

'Is that all?'

I collapsed back onto the sand.

Grace yawned, flung back her head restlessly. 'It is too hot. Where's Esther? Where that silly girl got to?'

Then Gracie surprised me by springing up and loping off to the shade of the *khonde* to be with Esther. I could hear them giggling together. I wondered if they were talking about me.

Mum and Dad stood on the shoreline, saying things like, 'Gosh, how amazing! Would you believe it? It's an old steam trawler from UK.'

The UK trawler came steaming up the lake, as if it belonged with crocodiles, flamingos, and girls whacking their washing on stones. It hooted to warn the canoes out there catching *chambo*.

'So how do you know it's from UK?' I asked Dad.

The blue beads in my hair clinked together, reminding me of the dance that night. Maybe, this time, I would get a boy.

'Those letters on the side, see, GY 126? She's from a fishing port in UK.'

That meant nothing to me. UK was an alien place. Sometimes my parents talked about the weather: 'Remember walking through autumn leaves? Remember icicles and snow?' But mostly they never spoke about UK. Their greatest fear was having to go back there.

I could see that this UK trawler, steaming up our lake, was really bothering them.

Dad said, 'She must have sailed from UK, been brought overland in bits then welded together on the shore of the lake. Amazing!'

The UK trawler chugged past flame trees and baobabs, scattering pink flamingos. Her decks were crammed with people, bicycles, baskets of stuff for market, maybe dried fish, green bananas, squawking chickens.

'Would you believe it?' said Mum.

But I knew they were scared. As if the trawler had come all the way to Africa to take them back to UK. They shouldn't have been here really. All the other white teachers, from UK, Canada, France, USA, had been sent back home. African teachers had taken their place. But somehow, my mum and dad had been overlooked.

The ferry went hooting off into the heat haze. But they stared after it, holding hands like two scared kids. As if they expected it to turn around and come back and get them.

I felt sorry for them. I thought they were a bit pathetic. They didn't belong anywhere. Not in Africa, even though they desperately wanted to. Or back in UK either.

Not like me. I was born here, at St Thomas's hospital just down the road. I didn't have any UK memories. I belonged to Africa. I felt as if I was one of its children—that this was my true home.

Mum let go of Dad's hand and turned round.

'I must see,' she fussed, 'whether those girls are cooking the cassava.'

She was a teacher again, grown-up, busy, busy, taking charge. Not a little kid scared by a big boat from UK.

7

She went bustling over to the *khonde*, where Esther and Grace were whispering secrets, to supervise the lunch.

Two

That night I was out on the beach with Esther and Grace, waiting for the dance at the Catholic boys' school.

I was feeling nervous. My belly was twittering like a treeful of weaver birds. Gracie had joked about getting me a boyfriend tonight.

'You've never had a boy *serious*, have you, Trish?' Gracie had teased me. 'You are still an innocent baby!'

No, I'd never had a boy serious. And I was fifteen already. I wondered about those girls in UK. Whether they would laugh at me for that.

Mum and Dad were in the mission house behind us. Soon, they would be sliding in under their mosquito nets. They always went to bed really early.

Esther and Grace and me had made a fire. Red sparks from our fire whisked off into the darkness. Out on the lake, they were night fishing. The fishermen's drums came across the water like soft heartbeats.

You could hear cries in the dark bush around us — strange whooping whistling noises. But I felt safe with my friends Esther and Grace, in our little circle of firelight, roasting maize and sweet potatoes.

We were telling stories. I knew stories, all African kids knew stories, about crafty hyenas, wicked snakes, wise hares, and stupid elephants. But the kind of stories Gracie knew, about spirits and devils and the walking dead—those were the kind of tales my parents never told me.

But Esther was telling her story first.

'And so,' said Esther, 'in the hot season the lazy spider sent his two sons out to search for food, while he stayed at home, getting drunk on *chibuku* in the shade of a jacaranda tree. And he told his sons: "My sons, I will tie this rope around my middle and whichever of you finds food first, that one must tug upon this rope and I will come to eat the food." So the two sons set out, one to the east, one to the west, and they were searching, searching. Then, in the east, the first-born found food and in the west at the same time, the second-born also found it. So they pulled and pulled, with mighty tugs upon the rope, both at the same time—'

'And that,' yawned Grace, 'is how spider got his nipped-in middle. And also it shows that you should not be lazy. It's a boring story, Esther. It is what teachers tell you in primary. It's my turn, OK? And this story I am telling you now is about a *witch*.'

Next to me Esther shivered with delight and dread. Grace stared into our eyes, as if she was hypnotizing chickens. She was a magical storyteller. The whites of her eyes glowed like two opals in the firelight. They had a strange expression in them. It was mischievous and contemptuous at the same time. As if to say: 'You are weak fools. for believing what I say!'

'On the shores of this lake,' Grace began, sweeping her arms about her, 'the people have seen balls of blue fire. They float just above the ground. They come at night and in the day. But mostly they come at night.'

'My uncle has seen them,' whispered Esther, her eyes bright with wonder.

'See,' said Grace. 'Esther knows I am speaking truth here.'

We crouched closer to the fire, throwing fearful glances behind us into the dark.

'Well, these fireballs, they are the property of a certain witch. They belong to her, personal. Some people even call them witch balls.'

Esther, who came from a lakeside village, spoke up again, 'This also is true,' she said, gravely.

Grace gave her an approving nod.

'Now this witch, she is very strange. She has long fingernails, very very long.'

Grace twisted her bony fingers in the firelight.

'Her nails are longer than porcupine spines. They are as long as a canoe, as long as that ferry boat we saw! They drag along the sand as she walks. Have you seen marks like these?'

With her nails, Grace dragged five trailing grooves in the sand beside her thigh.

I'd seen marks like that. But Dad said they were snake or lizard tracks.

'That is how you know she's around,' said Grace, smiling a sharkish smile. 'And then you must beware. For she is after kids just like you. Her fingernails are sharp like claws. And they go—' Here Grace clicked her fingernails right into Esther's face. '*Clack, clack.*'

Esther jerked back: '*Aieee!*' she shrieked, shivering.

'If you see those marks and if you hear that sound then you must run and hide!'

Grace smiled, smugly, this time. She knew she had us, body and soul, as easily as moulding rice balls in your hand.

'This witch I am telling you about—she lives on the shores of this very lake. She roams up and down, up and down. Sometimes she spears *chambo* with her fingernails. But most of all, she is fond of eating . . . *children.*'

'A child has disappeared from my village!'

'This witch likes fat children, fat as butter—'

'This one was fat as—'

'Shhhh!' I elbowed Esther in the ribs. 'Will you shut up?'

'And this is how she catches them. When a child sees

11

a witch ball he is frightened. He says to himself, "What is that thing?" ' And here, Grace mimicked a goofy boy. Someone giggled, shrilly. It was me.

'So he runs away, fast as he can on those fat legs. But that is a very wrong thing to do. Because the witch is waiting in the shadows and she traps him. *Clack!* Her long fingernails close round him like a cage.'

Grace made her own fingers into a cage.

'And this stupid boy is helpless. Her fingernails are round him like bars, he cannot escape. For although the witch's fingernails are white, like ours, they are stronger than iron. Children cannot break them. And the witch keeps the child inside until she feels,' and here Gracie leaned forward to leer into Esther's face, '*her belly getting hollow.*'

Beside me, I could feel Esther shudder.

'Do you know those birds, who keep lizards and little mice on thorns, until they are ready to eat them?'

I knew those birds. My dad had taken snaps of them. But I didn't answer because I could guess what was coming next.

'Well, this witch does that. She stabs the child with her long fingernails. She threads him on. He flaps like a fish caught on a spear. But he does not flap for long. Soon, he is dead. Sometimes this witch has two, three children on her nails. And that is very convenient, for she can carry her food around with her and take a piece . . . ' Here Grace's sharp white teeth crunched on a roasted maize cob, 'whenever she pleases.'

'That is a terrible story!' said Esther, her hands flying to her mouth.

'It is,' said Grace, nodding grimly. 'So if you see a witch ball, remember what I am telling you. Never run away because the witch will catch you for sure. Always run *towards* the witch ball, then you will be safe.'

Even I felt a cold sweat of fear between my shoulder blades—though I was so close to our fire it was scorching my legs.

'Rosebud must especially watch out,' added Gracie. 'She must look for signs in the sand and listen for *clack, clacks.* The witch will surely send her fireball for Rosebud.'

I laughed. Rosebud, our Head Prefect, daughter of the Minister for Agriculture, was prime witch bait. She had big thighs and meaty buttocks. I shifted my cramped legs. The story was over. Grace was suddenly bored with the game of terrorizing us, as if it was too easy to do.

She yawned. 'I am going to the dance now.'

Esther was still giggling in fear. But she begged, 'Tell us more stories about witches!'

'*Cha*, what babies you are. There are no witches,' Grace flung back at us over her shoulder.

I thought she winked at me then, choosing me above gentle, gullible Esther, as her special friend.

I smiled my best smile back at her.

Then she added one more thing. 'I forgot to tell you,' she said, looking straight into my eyes. 'That witch, the one I just told you about. She is a white witch. She has skin as white as a fish's belly.'

She did not say, 'Like yours.' But I felt that smile being wiped off my face. I felt bewildered and wounded, deep in my heart. But I wasn't sure why. It was only a story.

'That story,' said Esther, 'about that white witch. As for me, I do not believe it.'

'*Clack, clack!*' I told her cruelly, clicking my fingernails right in her face.

The soft glow of the hurricane lamps was spreading in Mum and Dad's bedroom. The electricity to the mission station had just gone off. It must be nine o'clock.

'You coming to this dance or not?' demanded Gracie.

I shone my torch to light up the path. The yellow eye bobbed in front of us, showing Gracie's feet, dusty in golden sandals. She had put on her best dancing shoes.

The boys' mission school, run by Catholic Brothers, was behind the mission house. It was built high on a mound like a red brick fortress. It had a massive monkey puzzle tree in front of it.

It was easy to find the dance. We just followed the sound of music on the jangly battery record player.

Hurricane lamps were swinging from the rafters of the school hall. Boys were dancing, shuffling in and out of swaying circles of light.

I saw straight away it was an unofficial Saturday night dance. That got me worried. At St Mark's the Saturday dances were strictly controlled. They ended at nine o'clock sharp. During the dance, teachers would patrol outside, checking the bushes with torches for couples making love.

But term time hadn't started yet. So there were no Catholic Brothers to police the dance, to shine torches in bushes. There were no other girls. Just some boys left behind in the school holidays, having a party on their own. You could smell *chibuku*—they'd been drinking. You could smell paraffin and beer and hot spicy sweat.

'Let's go,' I said to Esther. 'I don't like it here.' It smelled dangerous.

In the dark corners, I could see crowds of white shirts. I didn't know how many boys were in that room.

Someone asked me to dance. I was proud of my dancing. My parents had never got the knack of African music. They were too UK, too stiff and self-conscious. But I was a good dancer. That shuffle, sort of jerky but relaxed at the same time, came real easy to me. I was a natural.

14

But that night I couldn't relax. My dancing was *terrible*. My partner breathed *chibuku* fumes all over me. He said, 'I am real sexy, don't you think?' Then he said, 'How do you like our country?'

I mumbled some excuse and dodged away. He didn't even notice I'd gone. Just danced on alone, wriggling his hips, like I was still there.

Esther and Gracie were lost in the hot, crowded darkness. I was scared. I wanted to go home. I wished that the Catholic Brothers would turn up, flash torches around and take charge.

Then I found Gracie. I was rushing towards her when I saw she was dancing with someone. Boy, was he handsome, like a film star. He didn't look like a pupil to me—he looked like a teacher. He was still drunk though. I was disgusted at that—a teacher drunk! He was hanging on to Grace to keep himself upright, his feet slithering in the empty *chibuku* cartons on the floor. He was a lousy dancer. I spied on them from my shadowy corner. At school me and Grace were dancing partners. We'd won prizes in two school dancing competitions—two shillings to spend in the school tuck shop.

She must be hating it, dancing with him, I thought. A lousy dancer like that. No style. He couldn't win a shilling for the tuck shop.

But then they came staggering through the other dancers. They paused, swaying, right underneath a hurricane lamp. And I saw Grace smile up into the drunk face of her partner. I saw him squeeze her breasts and whisper in her ear . . .

I ran away. I didn't want to see any more. I stumbled past the monkey puzzle and down the dark track, forgetting to switch on my torch.

I was supposed to be sleeping in a tent on the beach with Grace and Esther. But I didn't go back there. I went back to the mission house. I felt my way into Mum and Dad's dark bedroom. They had separate beds. The ghostly cones of their mosquito nets hung down from the ceiling. I could hear their peaceful breathing from inside.

Something crunched. I jumped. I saw yellow eyes glaring at me. It was the mission house cat, eating a praying mantis. She didn't like their wings. She spat them out. In the morning, you'd find green mantis wings all over the floor like leaves after a storm.

I stood there, in darkness alive with sounds—breathing, crunching, things rustling in the thatch. Then I untucked one end of my mother's mosquito net. I slid in, clinging to the very edge of her mattress, so I didn't wake her.

I slept in Mum's bed that night, lulled by her gentle breathing. Smelling the rose petal scent of her hand cream that I remembered from when I was a baby.

PART TWO

ST MARK'S:
CHRISTMAS TERM

THREE

On Sunday, we left Zinja early and travelled home to St Mark's. Esther, Grace, and I squashed into the back of Dad's old VW, drinking warm Fanta, all the windows shut tight against the dust.

'Where did you run away to last night?' Gracie teased me. 'Did you find a boy? Did you let him take you into the bushes?'

I burst out angrily, 'You looked as if you found one. That handsome guy you were dancing with—'

'*Cha!*' Gracie threw her head back in disgust. 'That guy! I had only one dance with him. He was so *boring*! He said, "I teach Technical Drawing." Besides, he was very bad at dancing.'

I turned away, as if I was looking out of the window. But there was a secret smile spreading across my face.

We were almost back home, at St Mark's. We'd turned off the tarmac road onto a dirt track when suddenly there was a violent rainstorm. It sizzled on the hot metal of the VW. Even the windscreen wipers at full speed couldn't clear it. We crouched in the car, battered by the noise, like being inside a big drum. When it stopped the track streamed with red mud and the VW bounced about in the ruts.

'It's the rains,' said Esther. 'They've come early this year.'

Everything would grow really fast now. Our netball court at St Mark's would be hidden by yellow sunflowers. We'd have to hack through them with machetes before we could start our game.

'The girls will be arriving soon,' said Mum from the front seat. 'I can't believe Christmas term is starting already.' Her face looked tense and anxious, thinking of everything to do back at St Mark's.

Christmas term didn't start properly until Wednesday. But some of the girls would be setting out from their villages now. The poor ones would be walking all the way, for days through the bush, carrying cardboard suitcases on their heads. And in those suitcases would be—nothing. Maybe a comb or a piece of soap. When they got to St Mark's they'd get a school uniform, blue skirt, white blouse. They'd take off the dress they'd walked all the way in, fold it up in the suitcase and push the suitcase under their bed.

The rich ones would be flying in by plane, at the last minute, maybe from South Africa. They had all kinds of comforts, even their own radios. Rosebud, our Head Prefect, the Minister of Agriculture's daughter, would arrive in a sleek black Mercedes Benz with smoky windows.

The boys would be coming back too. But we only met boys for lessons, meals, and the Saturday night dance. The girls stayed up on the hill top. The boys slept in their own dormitories half a mile away. We talked a lot about the boys but we hardly ever met them. One girl who went creeping down the hill at midnight for a lover's meeting trod on a black mamba. She died. So lovers' meetings didn't happen often.

The VW was bumping past the main school buildings now—low concrete huts with tin roofs. You sweated in those huts in the hot season.

Suddenly Lovemore Jelenje walked out from amongst the tall grass. We nearly ran him over.

'A ha!' said Grace.

I felt her spark into life beside me. All the way back from Zinja she'd been sitting sulking, head drooping. Don't ask me why.

But Lovemore was always good for a laugh.

He was the school's Young Pioneer Instructor, about eighteen years old. He had a big green umbrella. That was to keep his uniform dry—his beautiful uniform, with creases like knives in the trousers. Mama Jelenje, his mum, slaved away with her charcoal-filled iron to get Lovemore turned out so smart. She was very ambitious for Lovemore. She wanted him to rise through Party ranks, become a VIP and visit her in her hut at the turn-off in a shiny black limo. Just like the one that drove Rosebud to school.

Dad rolled down the VW window. The air was fresh and cool after the rains. The crickets were chittering away like mad.

'*Moni*, Lovemore. How are you?'

'I am very fine today, thank you.'

'It has stopped raining, Lovemore,' Grace teased him, from the back of the car. 'Your nice uniform will not get wet.'

Lovemore struggled to put down his umbrella and got the spokes caught in his cuffs. A spray of raindrops spattered on his shirt. Lovemore pouted, his dignity wounded.

'Oh, Lovemore,' Grace mocked him. 'You are one sweet guy. Are you taking anyone steady? Will you take me?'

Lovemore backed off quickly, into the bush.

Beside me Grace was rocking with laughter.

Lovemore made notes on the conversations of students and teachers. In case they said something bad about the President. Or in case they talked about sex. Sex education was forbidden. We all knew about Lovemore, me and my friends. We knew he was a spy for the government. But we still couldn't take him seriously. He was a clown. And he was so pretty. He had long girl's eyelashes and a sweet face that was twitchy with nerves. He was an easy target. He carried a clipboard everywhere, trying to look really efficient. But the word was that he could hardly write.

Gracie said, 'I bet that boy didn't even get his Primary School Leaving Certificate! He is an ignorant village boy from somewhere up north! He is not educated, like us!'

Every morning Lovemore raised the flag at the school while we lined up behind him and messed around and tripped each other up when we were supposed to march off.

Mum and Dad always grovelled to Lovemore. That got me really mad. I raged at them. 'Don't you care? The way he spies and sneaks. Why are you so polite to him? All the students hate him!'

'You have to respect the rules,' Dad said.

'Nobody respects Lovemore. He's a joke.'

'Look, that boy represents the Government here. You and your friends shouldn't mock him the way you do. It's asking for trouble.'

I just laughed at that: '*Cha!* Trouble? What, *Lovemore?*' I didn't think Dad was being serious. St Mark's was the best school in the country. We were the best students. We really believed that made us safe.

On Monday, the day after we came back from Zinja, I was having breakfast with Esther and Grace on the *khonde* of Mum and Dad's bungalow.

This didn't happen often. When school started properly, I'd eat rice and beans in the dining hall, sleep in the dormitory, swap all the hottest gossip, just like one of the gang.

Augustus had bashed a piece of tin to tell us breakfast was ready. He was Mum and Dad's houseboy. He cooked, swept the bungalow floor with thorn twigs, did my mum and dad's washing.

I wouldn't let him do mine though. I washed my clothes in the big stone sinks in the shower block, same

22

as the other girls. Mum said, 'At least you should let Augustus iron them. Remember the putzi flies.'

Augustus was excellent at killing putzi fly eggs. He pressed the heavy iron into the seams of clothes, he killed every egg that was there. If you missed any, when you put your clothes on, the eggs burrowed under your skin and hatched out as fat yellow maggots. You could feel them wriggling as they ate their way out.

Mum said, 'They say putzi flies like white skin best.'

I said, 'You and Dad better watch out then.' I completely forgot I was white too, like them. I was always doing that.

The breakfast table was the same as always—a white and blue checked tablecloth, a bottle of malaria tablets, a big tin of Ricory coffee. Augustus clanged down our tin plates of porridge.

'Here is *nsima!*'

My parents had a box of Kellogg's cornflakes, bought from a shop in town where they sold UK food. They even had a jar of marmalade. But they didn't get these things out for Grace and Esther. It wasn't because they were mean. It was because they wanted people to think that they lived, like the rest of us, on rice, *nsima*, and red beans. But everyone knew about the UK food. Often I'd steal it from my parents, smuggle cornflakes into the dormitory where we'd eat them dry in handfuls. Sometimes I'd steal UK biscuits. My friends liked the ones called Nice biscuits because they had a hard sugary crust on top. I was really popular with the other girls when I stole those things from my parents' bungalow and shared them out.

My mum fished the husks out of her *nsima* and lined them up on the side of her plate. Why did she have to be so picky? None of us did that.

Esther chattered away to Mum: 'I think that the new girls will like our school, don't you?'

But Grace didn't chat. Gracie never felt obliged to be polite. She pushed her *nsima* round her plate. She was wearing copper bracelets that chinked every time she dug her spoon in. Her eyes looked blank and dead—there was no spark in them. I thought, What's wrong with her today?

Then I decided, She's bored stiff, having to eat with my mum. I grinned, to show her that I understood—that I was bored too. And I felt a rush of pleasure when her face gave me a brief, sparkling grin in reply.

It was already baking hot, even in the shade of the *khonde*. The kind of clammy, suffocating heat that leaves you gasping like fish in the bottom of a canoe.

'*Hodi!*'

Grace's head whipped round. She knew that voice: 'It is N'daka!' she said. 'He is back already!'

She sounded scared. But my ears must have been playing tricks. Gracie wasn't scared of anything. She especially wasn't scared of boys—not like I was.

That's another thing I wanted Grace to teach me—about boys. I couldn't go to UK to do A levels not knowing about boys. Those UK girls would laugh at me. They would think I was still a baby.

The gang of fifth form boys came swaggering up from school. Their leader was Matthew N'daka, tall with a handsome, proud face. Behind him was Gary from Rhodesia with his shades and psychedelic shirt, real cool.

Mum leapt up and challenged them as they came lounging up the track. Boys were not allowed on the hill where the girls lived. Not without a teacher's written permission. That was a very strict rule.

'What's your business, boys?' Mum asked them.

Mum's voice sounded bright and brittle. She was nervous. N'daka was trouble. He was a champion sprinter. Under his grey school uniform shorts, his

24

thighs swelled with muscles. He was the eldest son of an important Chief, full of swank, and he didn't like being ordered around by teachers, especially white, women teachers.

Once Gracie used to make fun of N'daka. She said his muscles filled his shorts but his head was empty as a basket going to market. But sometime last year she changed. She said, 'I hate that guy.' He must have upset her somehow. Of course, I didn't take it seriously. She was fickle like that with people, blowing hot one minute, cold the next. You never knew where you were with Gracie.

'Mr Chilolo sent us up here to move the beds,' explained Gary.

There was a storeroom a few yards down the hill where the bunk beds were stacked. They had to be carried to the dormitories and screwed together again before all the girls came back.

'Oh, that's wonderful!' exclaimed Mum, her voice all twittery with tension. The 'boys' always made her nervous when they were out of class. I'd noticed that. Some of them were shaving—some even had a wife and child back in their village. But Mum always spoke to them like little children. I mimicked her, in our dormitory, the way she twittered at the boys. My friends always shrieked with laughter—one day Esther even wet her pants.

N'daka ignored Mum, didn't even look at her. His head twitched like a restless bull. He had something on his mind.

'Off you go then, boys!' said Mum, clapping her hands at them, as if she was shooing chickens. 'I'll come down and supervise you in a moment. Just wait, Matthew. You seem to have appointed yourself leader. I'll give you the key. It's the most important job, looking after the key.'

I was squirming. She was trying to grease round N'daka. It was so obvious. I knew that. We all knew that. Even N'daka, with his head as empty as a basket, knew that.

I thought, That's pathetic.

In my mind I detached myself from her, as if I was coolly watching a stranger make a fool of herself, not my own mum. It wasn't hard. That's because I'd had lots of practice—I often looked at my parents through stern eyes, as if they were foreigners, nothing to do with me, not even the same colour.

'We not going,' said N'daka, flinging himself against the trunk of a crimson flamboyant tree. The others copied him, sprawling around him.

There was rain on the way. You could smell it. See it coming over the plains—grey columns, twisting madly between earth and sky.

N'daka eyed my mother. He didn't look angry. He even looked quite amused.

'Why aren't you going, Matthew?' asked Mum, getting all pink and flustered.

'It is woman's work,' N'daka told her, shrugging. 'Men don't carry.'

The boys with him got excited. 'He is right!' said one.

'And anyway,' said another. 'It is too hot.'

Gracie got up from the breakfast table. I thought the row would have perked her up—it looked like turning into something lively. But when I met her eyes, I saw that she looked really distressed, almost like she was in pain. I'd never seen her look that way before. It confused and upset me. I didn't know what it meant.

She was wearing her best blue and scarlet *zambia* and had another wrapped around her hair like a turban. It made her head look like a giant flower, too heavy for her neck to hold.

Still bewildered, I watched her take a few steps

towards our dormitory, then change her mind. She came back, sat hunched on the *khonde* steps, with her face away from the boys. She tucked her *zambia* in around her thighs and made room for me beside her. I was touched, thrilled that she should be so kind to me. I sat next to her.

'How are you, Gracie?' bellowed N'daka. 'Did you have nice days at Zinja?'

'Oh yes, very nice days,' she answered him. Only I, who sat so close, could feel her trembling.

Esther was very still, up in the shadow of the *khonde*. I could guess what she was up to. She was shovelling sugar into the big pockets of her school skirt, to sweeten her tea later. If she got the chance she would scoop out some Ricory coffee too. She could barter that for a sheet of green Croxley notepaper, an envelope, even a stamp to write a letter home to her mum. Esther was at St Mark's on a scholarship and her mum, a widow, was very poor. Esther never got any pocket money. She survived the best she could. I kept my eyes away from the *khonde*, to give Esther all the chances she needed.

'We will not carry beds,' one of the littlest boys told Grace proudly.

'*Cha!*' Grace turned to me but her bitter words were loud enough for everyone to hear: 'All men are like that. They are lazy, ignorant. They leave everything to the women.'

Behind me, on the *khonde*, I heard tiny clinking sounds—Esther shuffling the Ricory tin and sugar bowls around the table. Augustus, crouched on a grass mat at the other end of the *khonde*, had a clear view of Esther helping herself to madam's coffee. His face didn't show any expression at all.

I grinned at Augustus, to show him I shared the secret too. I felt a bond between us, Esther, me, and Augustus, as if the three of us were together, conspiring

27

against the *azungus*. But Augustus didn't grin back. He was looking at me, through me. His face was like stone.

Dad, who'd heard angry voices, came scrambling down from the bluff. He had a camera slung round his neck. There was a swimming hole up there, in the trees and Augustus had told Dad that a python, big enough to take a child, bathed there every morning. Dad had been trying for weeks to snap it. But it never came while he was there.

'They say they won't carry beds,' Mum complained to Dad. 'Even though Mr Chilolo told them they *must* do it.'

Dad's voice was calm, friendly, man-to-man. 'Come on, N'daka,' he said. 'Let's be reasonable. The beds are too heavy for these girls. They don't have muscles like you. They are weak.'

'That is true,' agreed someone at the back. The boys generally liked my dad. They saw *gudji-gudji*, who rushed here, there, even in the fiercest heat of the day, as a harmless fool.

'Shut your mouth, Chirwa,' said N'daka to the boy, without looking round.

'If you're not going to do anything,' said Mum, her voice getting shriller every second, 'then go back down to school.'

'We will screw the beds together,' announced N'daka, as if he was granting a very great favour. 'Do you have that screwdriver thing?'

He stared with easy contempt at my mum. N'daka rested mostly, or was waited on by his followers. They ran errands for him to the tuck shop, brought his breakfasts to the dormitory so he didn't have to eat in the dining hall. But he wasn't always idle. He had sudden, spectacular bursts of energy. He could go off, *whoosh*, like a firework. He could win races, if he felt like it. Or, if he felt like it, he could start a riot. He had the

28

power. Boys would follow him. Those from his village (it was a big, important village) *had* to follow him because his dad was Chief.

'We sorry and all that,' drawled Gary. He was good-humoured, apologetic. Gary was much richer than the rest of us. He wore fashionable clothes and shades, even indoors. He strummed the latest numbers on his steel-stringed guitar. He had it hanging round his neck now. Gary did not intend carrying beds today. His body was frail, slender. It looked as if carrying an iron bed would snap his bones. Anyway, he was too cool to carry beds, ever.

None of the boys were going to carry the beds.

But my parents just couldn't see it. Mum carried on greasing round them. Dad tried to jolly them along, 'Be reasonable, chaps!' It made me squirm.

Darkness hid most of the plain below us. Our hill was still an island of sunshine. But if you listened, you could hear a distant hissing noise, like a thousand snakes. That was rain coming.

What if N'daka started a bed-carrying riot? A school up north had been closed down by the government because of food riots. They said they didn't get enough to eat. So they burned down their classrooms with torches. A teacher died. But that was up in the uncivilized north at some third-rate secondary school buried in the bush. The government would never close us. We had excellent 'Cambridge' exam results. The sons and daughters of government ministers came here.

Still, I hated my parents for not standing up to N'daka. *Make* him carry the beds! I willed them. You're supposed to be teachers aren't you? You're supposed to be in charge of us.

But it was deadlock. N'daka was getting angry. He felt as if he'd been insulted—and that was when he was most dangerous. He was jabbing a finger at Mum and Dad, bawling at them.

It showed how bad things were getting because, when Gary lounged over to sit on the *khonde*, Mum didn't even notice. It was a school rule that pupils were not allowed to sit on the staff *khonde*—not unless they had special permission.

'I will report you to the headmaster,' Mum threatened N'daka.

N'daka laughed, a surprisingly high, girlish giggle. 'The headmaster is not here today,' he said. 'He is in town buying some new shoes. Anyway, you may tell him if you like.'

My mum tried bribery. She spoke to the other boys, not N'daka. 'You may have ten sweets each from the tuck shop if you carry beds,' she told them.

Two younger boys discussed this in urgent whispers. One said, 'May all my sweets be red ones?'

But N'daka shot them a poisonous look. He'd had enough.

'We will not carry beds!' he roared. 'These girls will do it!'

He jerked his bull head at the three of us sitting side by side on the *khonde* steps.

Esther had crept down to sit beside me and Grace. The pockets of her school skirt bulged out like stuffed pouches.

Then my mother did an unforgivable thing. She turned to us, her face twisting with nerves. 'What about it, girls? I'm sure you're not so stubborn. You'll show these lazy boys. You'll get the job done, won't you, without all this fuss?'

Esther got up to oblige.

'*No, Esther!*' Grace dragged her down again, roughly. Some of the Ricory coffee powder puffed in a brown cloud from her pocket.

But Grace wasn't even looking at Esther. She was staring straight into N'daka's eyes, her head held proud and high, but her lips trembling. 'We will not carry beds either,' she said.

'Ha!' said N'daka, in lordly disbelief. He turned to my dad, wagging his finger at him. 'You must tell these disobedient women. Tell them they must carry beds!'

I linked arms with Grace, to make it clear whose side I was on. 'I will not carry beds either,' I said, tilting my chin like Grace's.

Grace turned to me and in her eyes was a look of such fierce gratitude that it made me glow inside, bright as a million fireflies.

Dad said something calming. But Mum had a sort of mini breakdown. Clasping her hands, she swayed this way and that, as if her mind was playing tug-of-war with her body.

Then she made us all jump. She started shrieking, 'I'm sick, sick to death of the whole lot of you! We two,' and she swept her arm wildly in my dad's direction, 'will carry the beds! And you can all go to hell!'

N'daka clucked in disapproval. Secretly, I agreed with him. I didn't like Mum showing herself up, in front of my friends.

Mum went rushing off down the hill.

'She is a madwoman,' murmured Gary, gently strumming on his guitar.

My dad gazed after her as if he was scanning some distant horizon. 'Better go with her,' he said. His eyes met mine and he gave a sort of helpless shrug.

Grace had her arm round me. She drew me to her, as if she wanted to protect me. I lowered my head, avoiding my dad's eyes. I pretended to be scraping a thorn from between my toes, as if his troubles were none of my business. When I looked up again he was gone.

Mum and Dad dragged the beds up the hill all alone.

31

Mum was like a maniac, in a frenzy, heaving, pushing, her body straining with the effort. Dad looked resigned and trudged after her, lugging his end of the bed.

Grace spat out in disgust: 'Why did she give in? N'daka always takes what he wants, always. They should not let him do that!'

I was surprised that she sounded so deadly serious about it all. Grace wasn't often serious. She teased, she made fun, she didn't care about rules. I loved that about her. Even though, sometimes, it left my nerves ragged.

I was furious at Mum and Dad. I felt no pity for them, none at all, as they panted up and down the hill. I felt cruel and cold.

Maybe Mum thought, when we saw her struggling, that we'd rush to help. She should have known better. N'daka lost interest altogether.

'Let us go,' he yawned.

He wandered off, his followers jostling with each other to wave great cabbagy leaves over his head to keep the flies away.

They passed really close to my parents. Mum was pale and clammy and staggering; my dad sweating buckets. But N'daka and his gang never even glanced in their direction.

I didn't even pity them when the rain came sizzling down, drenching them in seconds, thundering off the tin roofs of the girls' dormitories, making the track down to school into a greasy yellow torrent.

'I am going now,' said Esther.

She went into the shelter of the dormitory to tip out her pockets and trade coffee and sugar with the girls that had already arrived. Then she would lie down on her bed and write a letter and send money home to her mum.

But Grace and I sat on the *khonde* until the bitter end. Watching my parents slithering in mud with the beds.

'Gary is right. That woman is mad,' commented Grace.

Mum's face was grim but triumphant. She really believed that she and Dad had won some kind of victory. But I knew better. I knew there would be more trouble ahead from N'daka. He wouldn't forget their loss of face.

At last the hissing sheets of rain hid Mum and Dad from view.

Then Augustus, who had been watching too, appeared and silently handed me a big, black umbrella. With our arms linked like sisters, Gracie and I walked beneath it across the compound to join Esther in our dormitory.

Four

Two days after Mum and Dad lost face in the bed-carrying incident, we found the head of one of Dad's nanny goats on our lawn.

Dad kept the goats for fresh milk. It was one of Mum's biggest complaints about Africa, that she couldn't get fresh milk to go in her tea.

Dad didn't have a clue about keeping goats. But he threw himself enthusiastically into it, like he did into everything else. But the goats strayed, they bit through their ropes, they broke into people's gardens and ate their young maize plants. Dad was always crashing through the bush trying to find them. Mum had already found a message pinned to the tree outside their bungalow: '*If you do not do something about your goats, something very bad will happen to them.*'

Mum said, when she found the note, 'Oh, it's not serious. No one will hurt our goats.'

I was in a bad mood that morning. They'd been drumming all night at the leprosy hospital down on the plain, so I hadn't had much sleep. Plus, I'd been forced to spend the night in the bungalow to be polite to Father Ignatius. He was white—an accountant and a Jesuit priest. Every year he came from South Africa to balance the school's books.

Mum said, 'He's such a polite, charming man!'

But Father Ignatius gave me the creeps. Behind his round, gold-rimmed spectacles, he had the robot eyes of a shark. He had creepy hands too—white, plump, with shiny nails as if he used clear nail varnish.

The night before, he'd been drinking my parents' sherry. Dad was checking on the goats. Mum had gone off with her torch to do the rounds of the girls' dormitories, checking for boys. I was on my own with him.

Father Ignatius's face was flushed. He leaned towards me, confidentially. I flinched back, I didn't know what to do. I began panicking inside—what if he put one of those plump white hands on my bare leg?

He breathed sherry fumes over me. His eyes glittered in their gold circles. He seemed very excited . . .

'Do you like numbers?' he whispered, leaning closer.

'Pardon?' I said, shakily.

'Do you like numbers? Do they thrill you at all? I find them beautiful, endlessly fascinating. Don't you agree?'

I shrank further back. I mumbled something, 'I'm no good at Maths.'

Father Ignatius's little shark eyes went dead again. His hand curled back round his sherry glass. He didn't pay me any more attention. I was very, very relieved.

Next morning—it was Saturday—I got up early to escape.

I was going to steal some bread, margarine, and some tinned apricot jam from the kitchen to take to the girls in my dormitory. I opened the front door first to check if it was raining.

That's when I saw the goat's head.

Flies were swarming round its white jelly eyes. Its blue tongue lolled horribly out of its mouth. Its pure white hair was streaked with blood.

There was a scream behind me. It was Mum. Then Father Ignatius slid up to the door. He glanced out.

'It's one of our goats!' Mum explained, her voice trembling, her hands flying to her mouth in horror. 'Who would do such a thing?'

'Ach, these natives,' said Father Ignatius, shaking his head and smiling.

As soon as I got to my dormitory I found out who had

killed the goat. All the girls knew; they were all talking about it. Soon everyone knew but Mum and Dad. It was Augustus. The girls had seen him put the head on the lawn.

They told me Augustus had lost all his maize crop because of Dad's goats. That they had broken into his garden and eaten all the tender young shoots. That he had borrowed money for fertilizer and now there would be no maize to sell so he couldn't pay the money back. It was a disaster for him.

'And now his baby will go hungry,' said Reen Tambala. 'Its belly will be swollen.' I never knew Augustus had a baby. I'd never even given it a thought.

I felt bitter anger towards my dad. He knew his goats were a nuisance. But he had no idea of the terrible trouble they caused. I blamed him totally for what had happened. For driving Augustus to do something desperate.

It was a very pretty goat. Its name was Celeste. I thought how shocked Mum and Dad would be if they knew Augustus had done it. They were convinced they had a really good relationship with Augustus. I thought again what blind fools they were. They didn't understand things. They didn't belong here. Not like I did.

Gracie was lying on her iron cot. She was reading *Forum*, the school magazine that Mum edited.

'Truly, this is a boring magazine!' she said. 'It is always saying about rules! For heaven's sake, that fool Z. Zayamakanda has written about how important it is to pick up litter and keep the place tidy now that St Mark's Day is near! "Remember that it is a school rule to be tidy", he says. Ha!'

Gracie ripped up her copy of *Forum* and scattered it all over the floor.

St Mark's Day, on November 19th, was the most important day of the year, when we celebrated the founding of our school.

'I hate St Mark's Day,' said Grace. 'It is boring too.'
She yawned. '*Eeee*, I am bored out of my brains at this
place.'

'I know!' said Reen Tambala. 'Let us go on a picnic to
the swimming hole.'

'We don't have a teacher's permission,' I said, before
I could stop myself.

'*Cha!*' Grace rolled her eyes in exasperation. 'What a
good little Missy you are!'

I blushed. 'No, I'm not.' And to prove it I said, 'I'll
go and steal some stuff from our kitchen.'

Back at the bungalow, the goat's head had been tidied
away. But my parents were still very upset. My mum kept
asking, like a bewildered child, 'Who'd do something like
that?' She turned to me. 'Do the girls know who did it?'

I shook my head solemnly. 'No, nobody knows
anything at all.'

The goat's head was gone. But Mum and Dad kept
sneaking glances outside. As if they were under siege. As
if they half-expected some other bloody head to appear
on their velvet-green English lawn.

Mum seemed to be numb, in a daze. She said to Dad,
'They killed a baby baboon last rainy season. Do you
remember that, John?'

'That's got nothing to do with this, Cissy,' said Dad,
trying to calm her down. 'And anyway, we know who
did that. Esther did that.'

Now, that had really, *really* shocked my mum. Seeing
gentle, timid Esther howling like a wild dog and
chucking stones at the baboon baby screeching in the
flamboyant tree.

'Stop it, Esther. How could you be so cruel?' Mum
had yelled at her.

Mum never got over it. Which is one reason I didn't
try to explain about Augustus and the goat. I'd explained
it all before and she hadn't listened then.

37

'You don't understand, do you? You'd hate baboons as well if you had a garden here,' I'd told her. 'Gangs of them go wild, wreck your crops, just for the fun of it. They don't even eat it. People starve cos of them. Babies starve! You'd kill them too whenever you got the chance.'

But she'd just said: 'You saw what Esther was doing. Why didn't you stop her? You were watching—'

I wasn't actually. As a matter of fact I'd closed my eyes and put my hands over my ears to cut out the sound of its shrieking.

They were still talking about the goat when I stole the food from the kitchen. They couldn't seem to stop talking about it. That and the bed-carrying incident had really upset them, as if they'd been given some kind of dreadful warning. Mum told Dad, 'John, I feel as if things are falling apart all around us.'

Father Ignatius just shrugged. 'Ach, these natives. What else do you expect?'

I left them to it. It was their business, their mistakes. I had my own life, separate from theirs. I was beginning to feel that speaking to them, even being seen with them, was compromising me somehow. I belonged with my friends, in my dormitory, not with them. I wanted everyone to be perfectly clear whose side I was on.

On my way back, with my arms full of food for the picnic, I suddenly caught sight of someone in Reen Tambala's mirror, hung on a nail over her bed. I thought resentfully, What's that white girl doing here? Until I realized, with my usual shock, that it was my own face I was staring at.

Esther came in, with a cooking pot. 'Did you get the record player?' she asked me. I had stolen the battery record player and some records from the locked cupboard where Dad kept it. I'd return it later, without him even knowing it was gone.

Gracie leapt up from her bed scattering more pieces of *Forum*. She had plastic flip-flops on that looked as if they were made of clear, pink candy. She had plaited her hair with red cotton. The copper bracelets clinked on her arm.

'Let us go then!'

Gracie was in one of her best moods ever. And when she was like that I was her willing slave. There was a heady freedom about her. I wanted to be like that— reckless, brave, disdainful, saying '*Cha!*' to the rules. I thought I could learn those things from her. Maybe I even thought she'd give them to me, like a present.

Yet even I had to admit that Gracie had changed a lot over the last year. Sometimes she seemed as solemn and weighed down with care as Rosebud, Head Prefect and Minister of Agriculture's daughter.

'Hey,' said Lily, who was light-skinned and one quarter Portuguese. 'We better watch out for that python.'

'I forgot about that,' I said, alarmed. 'Maybe we shouldn't go. Augustus told Dad he'd seen a python there, big enough to take a child.'

They all laughed at me. Bewildered, I searched their faces. 'There is a python, isn't there?'

'That was a lie,' said Grace. 'You didn't believe it, did you?'

'No, no, 'course I didn't. But why did Augustus tell that lie?'

'Because he knew that *gudji-gudji* would believe it,' said Lily. 'And that he would take his camera up there and wait around in the hot sun to snap this champion snake.'

I laughed too. We all laughed together. '*Azungus* will believe anything!' giggled Lily.

But then I just had to blurt out, before I could stop myself, 'So there isn't a python up there then?'

'There is,' said Gracie, flashing her eyes at me, 'and he eats children. And you are such a skinny little baby that he will swallow you whole.'

The swimming hole was half a mile or so up the bluff. There was no path through the bush but there was a water pipeline. So we had to walk along that.

The pipeline was covered in heaps of stones to protect it. I stumbled on the stones, tripping, trapping my feet between them, sending them skittering back down the bluff, while Lily walked in front of me with the record player balanced on her head, never once faltering. Somewhere in the file of girls someone had the records wrapped in a cloth. Someone else had the sugar and tea from our kitchen. I was always invited on picnics.

'We are here at last,' said Grace dropping down on the hot rocks.

It was easy to believe that pythons bathed in our swimming hole. Rocky cliffs, dripping with ferns, rose sheer on either side. The pool was clear, deep with a bottom of pebbles and sand. Little waterfalls gushed in and out of it and tiny rainbows, blue, violet, and orange, flitted like humming birds over it.

Only Reen had a bathing suit. The rest of us stripped off our school uniform and dived in in our underwear. We went crazy, shrieking, splashing like little kids. The cool water on our sticky, hot bodies made us shiver with delight. I dived down. The sand at the bottom crunched between my toes. Then I shot up into shimmering rainbows, shaking water drops off my hair. The gorge rang with shouts and laughter. Fuzzy honey-coloured monkeys with dark faces ran away, whooping alarm calls.

We doggy-paddled about—all of us did the doggy paddle. We didn't know how to swim any other way.

After a while we got tired. Our shouts faded. Esther got out of the pool, lit a fire, roasted groundnuts. She made a cooking pot full of very sweet tea with tea leaves and blobs of powdered milk floating on top. We dipped our tin mugs in it. It tasted like heaven.

We put records on—Reen and Lily clung together, dancing lazily to the tinny music.

Grace had draped herself on a sunny rock, to dry her underwear. I edged towards her. The other girls were stirring cabbage and tomatoes in the cooking pot. Or drifting dreamily in the pool, their eyes closed. The batteries in the record player had run down. The sun had moved round and the gorge flickered with warm, green shadows. It was so still. Even the crickets had stopped chittering.

To be truthful, Grace had never taken *much* notice of me. But, lately, she'd taken no special notice of me at all.

So I was really startled, as I crept closer, when she sat up, clasped her arms around her knees and stared straight into my eyes.

'How are you these days?' she said to me.

'I'm . . . I'm fine.'

'I have not been a good friend,' she said.

She sounded irritated rather than sorry. But her use of the word 'friend' was like giving water to someone dying in a desert. 'I have many troubles,' she added. But I hardly noticed that bit. I was too busy treasuring the word 'friend', turning it round and round like a sparkling jewel in my mind.

Then she said the most amazing thing of all. 'I have an idea. Why don't you spend some days at my house?'

I felt my heart stop dead, then jolt into life again.

'What did you say?'

'I said, "Why don't you spend some days at my house?" You could come there in the Christmas holidays.'

'Really?' I said. 'Do you *really* mean it?'

'For sure! I have just said it, girl.'

I was still stunned, disbelieving. As I opened my

mouth to say something, somebody screamed. It almost seemed as if the sound was coming from my lips—

'Look, *askari*!' someone shouted.

Above us the bushes were moving. The scrubbed slopes swarmed with creeping soldiers. There were green leaves shaking on their helmets. They wore camouflage gear and heavy black boots. And they carried guns.

'They have come to get us!' cried Esther, cowering against the rocks.

Some had seen us. Through the spray, the rainbows of the waterfall, we saw three of them crouching on the edge of the gorge, peering down. They were young for soldiers, maybe the same age as me. Their helmets were too big for them. They weren't smiling, or even leering at us in our underwear. Their faces had a sinister look— blank and frozen. As if they were waiting for an officer to tell them what to do.

I wondered how long they'd been spying on us. Whether they had seen Reen naked, when she changed into her bathing suit behind the rocks. I began to be very afraid.

A weird figure, a green man wreathed in trembling leaves, shot up from the bush, threw something overarm and sank down again. Then another shot up, then another and another.

'They've got grenades!' I cried out, in English. Then I crammed my fist into my mouth to keep myself quiet.

Behind me, Grace giggled. My head whipped round. I thought she'd become hysterical.

'They have no grenades,' she said. 'They are pretending.'

'What you *talking* about?'

'Just use your eyes, girl. See, they move their arms but throw nothing.'

It was true. They had no grenades, no bullets.

'Look,' giggled Reen. 'Their guns are like toy guns. They are made of wood!'

They were boy soldiers on manoeuvres, making a pretend attack on an imaginary enemy. One dropped down on his belly and sniped at a fig tree.

'Bang,' I said.

I was giggling like mad as well. It was comical. It seemed to me the funniest thing I'd seen. Stupid boys in big boots, their pin heads rattling around in big helmets, sneaking through the bush, playing soldiers.

They moved on. The three at the edge of the waterfall melted into the bush. In seconds the gorge was ours again.

'They've gone. What idiots.'

'Perhaps they have gone to attack St Mark's,' said Lily. 'Your mother will just tell them, "No boys on the *khonde*". She will say, "You can't go to the turn-off unless you have a pass!"'

Only Esther, her teeth chattering, seemed paralysed, clinging to the rocks like a starfish.

'They've gone Esther,' I told her, impatiently. 'It's OK now.'

Esther had always been timid—but this was over the top, even for her.

'They've *gone*. What's the matter with you?'

'Oh, she is like that because they took her father,' Grace said, casually, as if it was nothing uncommon. '*Askari* like that took him. Didn't you know? They came and took him away in the night.'

'I didn't know that,' I said, shocked to the core. 'Why did they take him?'

'Who knows? He joined a strike at his bakery, I think. He is dead now. He died in prison. They told Esther's mum he died quickly of fever. But they would not let her see his body.'

'Why—?'

'They took her brothers as well,' added Grace. 'All her brothers. On that same night.'

'No one told me about any of this . . . '

I wanted to ask more questions but my friends were busy. Tenderly, carefully, they were prising Esther from the rocks. Loosening the grip of her hands, finger by clutching finger.

Then they supported her, a weeping tragic figure, all the way back to school.

'Hey,' I shouted after them. 'Someone help me with this record player. Dad will go crazy if he doesn't get it back!'

But none of them helped me. They left me behind to struggle down the pipeline alone.

FIVE

On the morning of November 19th, St Mark's Day, I
was in Mum and Dad's bungalow. I'd hardly spoken to
my parents, hadn't been to their bungalow for days, not
since the picnic at the swimming hole. I was only here
now because I'd come to steal some sugar.

The visit to Grace's village was all I thought about
these days. It was all fixed up—I was going at Christmas.
And for two weeks I'd have Gracie's whole attention,
instead of the scraps I'd got so far. I thought my special
invitation would make us closer. But Gracie took no more
interest in me than she had before. Sometimes it was hard
to believe I was actually going—that I hadn't dreamed
up the whole thing. I had to find ways of bringing it into
the conversation, just to reassure myself that the
invitation was for real.

'What will we do, when we go to your village?' I'd
asked her.

'Oh, we have lots of entertainment. We can go for
cinema, for swimming—life is fun, fun, fun there.'

'You have a *cinema* in your village?'

'No, I was lying, of course. It is boring, all villages are
boring! But don't worry, we will have happy times there.'

It struck me that I knew nothing at all about Grace's
life outside St Mark's.

'When we go to your village,' I'd asked her, 'will I see
your brothers and sisters?'

'Oh yes, you will be tripping over them. They will
drive you crazy.'

But she didn't give me any more information about
her family. And questions made her impatient. So I
didn't ask them often.

By St Mark's Day morning, Mum was worn out. She'd been busy for weeks, getting ready, organizing, rushing about in the hot sun, ticking things off her lists. Mum took St Mark's Day very seriously—much more seriously than any of us.

She pointed to her lip, 'Doesn't this look frightful? And on St Mark's Day too. The most important day in the school year.'

Her bottom lip was bright purple. The nurse at St Thomas's had painted her cold sores with gentian violet.

I was hardly listening. I wasn't interested. I turned to look out of the window—And there was a bloody goat's head on the lawn! Horrified, I screwed my fists in to my eyes, blinked and looked again.

It wasn't there, of course. I'd just imagined it. There was only the cat, striped like a little tiger, spitting out mantis wings.

I looked beyond the lawn, trying to calm myself down. The plain was misty this morning. Far, far away, you could see mountains rising out of the white haze like the spiny backs of sea monsters—

My mum screamed.

'John! John!'

'What's the matter? Dad's not here. You just told me. You said he'd taken that boy to the leprosy hospital.'

'Scorpion!' said my mum pointing.

It had fallen out of her shoe. Everyone, automatically, tapped their shoes out before they put them on.

'Augustus!' she yelled.

Augustus did not come. But I knew he was just outside, relaxing on the straw mat on the *khonde*.

The giant black scorpions were not so dangerous. Their poison was no worse than a bee sting. But this tiny brown one was deadly. Its sting could kill you.

Its armoured body reared instantly into the threat

46

position. Mum whacked it with her shoe, grunting with each blow like a fighter.

'*Ugh! Ugh! Ugh!*'

I'd never seen my mum so violent, heard her make ugly sounds like that. She was going berserk.

The scorpion was twisted, crushed. But it wasn't dead. Scorpions were practically indestructible. They could even survive fire.

Mum pounced again. She smashed it, taking careful aim, using the heel of her shoe as a hammer.

'Why . . . don't . . . you . . . die!' she panted.

Then she backed off, to see what damage she'd done. I watched her, half-amused, half-horrified. I'd never seen her behave like this—let her feelings out so savagely. It wasn't like Mum at all.

The scorpion was thrashing about, mortally wounded. It killed itself, stabbing itself in the back again and again with its own sting. At last it quivered and lay still.

At that very moment, Augustus lounged in with a dustpan and brush. He must have been watching. Without a single word he swept the scorpion's mangled body into the dustpan, took it outside, and tipped it over the edge of the *khonde*.

'That's got rid of that,' said Mum.

She stood trembling, her shoe dangling from her hand. Her hair had tumbled out of its French pleat, all her hairpins were on the floor. Her lists for the organization of St Mark's Day, for the inter-house games, the prize giving, the film show and dance this evening, had fallen off the desk.

I didn't like it. It was worse than the bed-carrying incident. She was like a mad woman with her long, wild hair and her freaky purple lip.

I thought, She's cracking up. I went running back to my friends in the dormitory. I didn't even hang around long enough to steal the sugar.

When I saw her half an hour later in the school chapel I was relieved to see that, apart from that lip, she looked like she always did. Her hair was neat again. All the hairpins were back in it. She looked efficient and in control, with her clipboard full of lists.

St Mark's Day started off with fifteen minutes of calm. I loved the school chapel. It was dim inside, peaceful, cool. It had just been thatched and the yellow straw smelled fresh and warm like baking bread. We knelt on grass mats. I was next to Grace. We all sang our National Song together. Grace had a high, shaky singing voice—a weird kind of voice for someone as fiery and tough as she was.

Mr Jawali the headmaster spoke to us. He was a tiny, mild, birdlike man. So soft-spoken I couldn't hear much. I couldn't help staring at his smart new shoes. They were black and shiny like ebony. It must have been true what N'daka said—that he had been to town to buy shoes. How did N'daka know that? Maybe, I thought, Mr Jawali has to have N'daka's written permission to go to town, like we have to have Mr Jawali's to go to Mr Khan's shop at the turn-off.

Then we tumbled out of chapel into the bright sunshine. And the real business of St Mark's Day, the team sports, began. There were four teams, green, red, blue, and yellow. Gracie and I were in blue.

The day got hot very quickly. The football field was parched and crispy brown—it was always like that, even in the rainy season.

Danny Nyong'onya, our team's best runner, was loping home from the long-distance race. The other runners were still somewhere up the bluff but Danny had barely worked up a sweat. He was wearing the regulation PE kit—white wrinkled cotton shorts and vest. But he had a striped scarf tied around his head.

'Agnes is going out with Nyong'onya,' said Grace. 'She is taking him steady. That is her scarf he is wearing.'

'I think he's a handsome guy, don't you?'

'*Cha!* He is a baby. He hasn't started shaving yet. His chin is not even fertile.'

I watched Agnes do the high-jump, arching her lean body backwards over the cane.

'Are these games finished yet?' yawned Gracie.

Gracie and I were sprawled on the edge of the football field drinking warm Fanta.

All around us were jungly hills, bright green after the rains.

'They finish at twelve o'clock for lunch and prize-giving. There's some VIP coming to give the prizes, a Minister or someone like that. Isn't it Rosebud's dad?'

Grace swatted the flies away. 'Oh, probably.'

I was a useless athlete—I wasn't entered for anything. But Gracie was good. She had just run the relay, the only race she'd agreed to enter. My mum couldn't understand why she wouldn't run around in the blazing sun playing netball. 'What about loyalty to your team? Don't you care about that at all? You're letting us all down you know,' she nagged Gracie.

I knew Gracie didn't want to—but I sort of half-wished she'd enter more races. I loved watching her win races. It thrilled me to see her power down the home straight, burning up the track, then just toss the baton aside as if to say, '*Cha!* It is nothing.'

Some people from the turn-off had wandered onto the field—women with babies slung on their backs, children whirling their skinny arms and legs copying the athletes. Next to us, a woman was feeding her baby. It was snuffling against her breast. I wasn't interested in babies but Gracie went up to its mum, 'How old is he?' she asked her.

Then Gracie came back to me: 'That baby is the same age as our last born, Heston.'

'I didn't know you had a baby brother.' It was the first time she'd willingly told me anything.

I made my voice bright, eager, wanting her to tell me more about the family I'd be spending Christmas with. But she fell into a dream and said nothing. Both of us were getting woozy with the heat.

'The games are finished,' said Chirwa, who was sitting near us. 'I want my lunch.'

We were all hungry, thirsty. There was no shade on the football field.

We'd had nothing to eat since a tin plate of maize porridge at 6.30. The VIP was very late. The weather was getting stormy—a fierce, hot wind was whipping up dust devils all over the field.

'My belly is rumbling!' shouted Chirwa. 'And I am too hot!'

In one corner of the field was a green military-style tent. We were all watching that tent, our eyes never left it. There were buckets of tea outside, growing cold. And on benches, under white cloths, was food to be shared out. Two scones, two slices of bread and tinned jam, a banana, a Fanta, and six sweets. We all knew exactly what we were entitled to.

'We hungry,' growled N'daka. He sounded dangerous. 'Why must we wait? This is not right!'

At 1.45 a Mercedes Benz, its glossy blackness spoiled by red dust, came jolting over our football field. Behind it was an open lorry, stuffed with fat mamas. They were wearing the official Party colours, yellow and green. They were cheerleaders for the Minister.

Teachers sprang into life, herding us towards the prize-giving platform. I could hear my mum's nervy voice. 'Come on, students. Hurry, hurry, the Minister is behind schedule. He is late for his next appointment.'

'Is that Rosebud's father?' I asked Esther, as we shuffled into place round the platform.

'I don't know, I have never seen him.'

'We hungry,' growled N'daka again, his great bull-head nodding in the direction of the lunch tent. He sounded as if he was in a very bad mood. 'We should have lunch now! That guy should make his speech after we have eaten!'

The Minister looked sharp in his black suit and shades. But he gabbled through his speech at top speed. The microphone screeched and buzzed, we couldn't make out a word. The mamas warbled and clapped and danced.

'*Ululululu!*'

Lovemore, his trouser creases sharper than we'd ever seen them, pushed a little boy up to take his Young Pioneer Oath. But when the boy froze with fear, the mike was snatched away so the Minister wouldn't be held up.

We fidgeted, watching that lunch tent. Our stomachs were cramped with hunger. Many students had fainted already. Teachers were laying them out in rows like dried *chambo* at the edge of the field. Dad was back from the leprosy hospital. I saw him helping Esther, who'd slumped to the ground.

I felt pretty dizzy and sick myself. The sun was cruel. But black clouds were massing in the north—that meant rain. The people from the turn-off knew that. They didn't have to stay to hear the Minister; they were already heading for shelter.

'We have worked hard!' protested someone. 'We have done running, jumping. Where is our reward?'

'Must we have just *two* scones?' someone else said. 'It is not enough. We are famished!'

Saliva, gritty with dust, pumped into my mouth at the thought of food.

'And now,' the Minister shrieked through the mike, 'you must all run up here to receive your prizes, for I am very late.' He said it accusingly, in a bad-tempered voice, as if we were to blame.

'Frank Mbereko, first in long jump. Come on, quickly,' called Mr Chilolo. 'Run, run!'

Someone yelled, 'They are taking the lunch tent away!'

We all rushed for the tent in a trampling scrum, leaving the Minister on the platform speaking to no one. Teachers struggled to protect the food.

I could hear Dad pleading, 'Now come on, be reasonable.'

But we grabbed all we could get, stashed some inside our vests to eat later.

'Eeee, I have got four scones!' someone shouted, right into my face.

There was no fighting. We helped each other to food. But, by the end, the tent was a toppling wreck and the benches stripped even of crumbs.

Some blue tuck shop sweets had been stamped into the dirt—they glowed like sapphires. Little Lily was crouched in a whirl of legs prising them up with a stick.

My mum flapped about, crying out in outrage and despair. 'You must take *two* scones! Only *two* scones are allowed!'

No one listened. Her neat hair had tumbled down again. I saw Esther, who felt better now, swooping on the shed hairpins. I knew what she wanted them for. She would use them, later, to mend her only pair of flip-flops.

While Mum went frantic, Mr Chilolo and the other teachers backed off, letting the 'food riot' run its course. Some teachers found it a good time to go home for lunch.

When everyone had snatched something, the raid on the food was instantly over. A hundred students lounged on the football field, laughing, chatting, swapping sweets for banana, bread for Fanta, as if it had never happened.

Then someone finally noticed, 'The Minister has gone . . . '

The Mercedes Benz, the gang of yellow and green mamas, the gun-toting bodyguards, had all disappeared. The VIP platform was empty. Only the headmaster was up there, looking miserable, in his best safari suit. The first drops of rain fell, big as pennies, splashing his beautiful shiny new shoes.

Lovemore looked tragic. For weeks he had been training a gymnastic display team to entertain the VIP. His team was cooped up behind ropes in a corner of the field, still hungry, thirsty. They hadn't joined the stampede for food.

Lovemore gazed along the red track, as if he couldn't believe it. His big moment, his big chance to impress a VIP from the government, had vanished with that limo.

Tears sparkled on his long lashes. He was inconsolable. His gymnastic team watched their leader trudge off into the bush, his clipboard drooping from his hand.

They were so well drilled that they stayed behind their ropes, penned up like cattle, while the rain hissed down and turned their little corner into a swimming hole.

SIX

On the afternoon of St Mark's Day, the dining hall cooks went on strike because the house boys, like Augustus, had been given a bonus for extra work. They refused to wash up after the teachers' tea of egg and tomato sandwiches. They refused to cook the students' rice and beans.

'How could they strike on St Mark's Day?' said Mum. She just couldn't understand it.

So Mum washed up a toppling mountain of plates and cups and teaspoons, while Esther and Rosebud the head prefect helped her and sang cheery songs.

Grace and me saw them through the windows of the kitchen.

'Does that woman never rest?' grumbled Gracie. 'She will wear herself out.'

But Mum was saved from making rice and red beans in the huge cooking pots because Dad slipped the cooks five shillings each out of his own pocket without telling her.

Someone said they'd seen Lovemore up a baobab tree near the turn-off. Even his mum, Mama Jelenje couldn't coax him down. She warned him about boomslangs, sneaking along the branches, but he didn't listen. Even when a crowd of little kids gathered to tease him he just peered miserably down at them. Then climbed higher and burrowed out of sight among the leaves.

'You coming or what, girl?' Grace asked me.

It was dark and all the girls were on their way down the hill for the film show and school dance afterwards. These were the last events in St Mark's Day.

'Wait a minute, I forgot my torch.'

After I got it from the dormitory, I had to run to catch up with the others. I could hear their excited chatter disappearing down the track.

Light from the window of Mum and Dad's bungalow was spilling out onto the lawn. For some reason I crept closer and sneaked a look in, like a peeping Tom.

They were sitting on their yellow plastic settee. Dad said something to Mum. She turned to him and smiled. He folded his arm around her and they cuddled up close. This should have made me squirm. I mean, normally it would have. But that night I didn't feel like that. It shocked me, how I felt. I wanted to be included in that loving moment. I felt a desperate longing to rush in, force my way in between them and say, 'Hug me too.' I wanted to do that so badly, it hurt.

But then someone's voice yelled from out of the darkness, 'Where are you, Trish? We waiting for you!'

I turned away from my parents' window and followed the other girls down to school.

They'd set the cine screen up in the open air. The rain had stopped and above us the sky was cloud-free and navy-blue, fizzing with shooting stars. We had been promised an action film—a film from USA about spies. There were more than one hundred people sitting cross-legged in the compound with the chapel and rows of low, brick classrooms closing us in.

There was not much noise. We shuffled around while Mr Chilolo fixed the projector. It was always breaking down. We ate food. That was the most important thing about St Mark's Day—the extra food rations. Mary Kainja crunched sugar cane. In her lap was a pile of roasted groundnuts. Chirwa was eating fried locusts, threaded on a stick.

55

The night air was fruity with the smell of oranges. Everyone had been given an orange and two biscuits after supper in honour of St Mark's Day.

'When is this film thing to start?' said someone from the back.

The projector whirred into life.

Mum and Dad had come down from the hill. They were on duty—again. They were standing together by the screen. Mum's purple lip glowed in the dark like neon. She was worried, her eyes flickering everywhere. She and Dad were expecting more trouble. I heard them discussing it.

'Those disgraceful scenes on the football field,' Mum said, shaking her head. 'I just don't know what came over them. I'm not surprised the Minister left in a hurry. It'll be a black mark for the school, there's no doubt about that.'

The giant shadow of an insect, caught in the light beam from the projector, loomed at us. It waved feelers as big as palm fronds. Lily said 'Ahhhhh!' She clapped wildly. She'd never seen a film—she thought it had already started.

Gracie chuckled and shook her head, 'That uneducated girl . . . '

A soupy grey picture trembled on the screen, just for two seconds. We cheered. But then the screen went blank again. So we waited . . .

I nudged Grace in the ribs.

She was lining up orange segments along her bare leg. She looked up. 'What is happening?'

'I think that stupid projector isn't working again.'

'This is boring!' someone yelled.

Grace was working her way up her leg eating the orange segments one by one. She flicked the last one over her shoulder. 'Eeee, I have eaten too much,' she said, rubbing her belly.

A puzzled bellow came from the back. 'Where is our film?' It was N'daka.

I could see my mum's neck craning like a hare out of a maize field, trying to pick N'daka out in the crowd.

'Never mind,' said Mr Chilolo, mildly. 'We will view it some other time, as soon as the projector is mended. Meanwhile, there is more time for dancing.'

Dance music, jangling from the school hall, lured us inside. But many of us were complaining loudly. 'We were promised a film!'

N'daka was shouting, 'Where is our film?' even after the screen had been rolled up and the projector taken away.

I loved dancing—sweating, feeling my body shake itself loose, as if I was melting into the floor. After the first record Gary came slinking over. I often danced with him at school dances, when I wasn't dancing with Grace. He was a really good dancer. But tonight I smelled *chibuku* on his breath. He must have been down to the turn-off. That wasn't allowed. If Mum found out she would put him on report.

He draped his arms round my neck. I pushed him away. 'No, I don't like to dance close. I'd rather dance on my own.'

'Oh,' pouted Gary. 'Haven't you got the hots for me? You are not romantic . . . '

He drifted off. I danced with Grace.

I kept sneaking glances at her. She was wearing a new *zambia*, a very splendid one—dark green, gold, and black. In the last week two parcels had arrived for her from her village. We had all crowded round her and sighed, '*Aieee*,' when the rich cloth spilled out on her dormitory bed.

'Who sent them, Gracie?' I asked her.

But it was maddening, she only gave secret smiles and stored the *zambia* away in the suitcase under her bed.

I guessed that Grace's parents had sent her these presents. I was relieved to know she had rich, generous parents. I'd started to feel a bit uneasy about spending Christmas at Gracie's house. I was used to the safety of St Mark's—lights out at 9.30, no mixing with boys. Even though I'd been born here, at St Thomas's, I'd never stayed overnight with an African family.

I still wanted to go. 'Course I did. It proved Gracie liked me best of all. She'd invited me—not Lily or Reen or Rosebud or even Esther. It made me special. The only trouble was, she didn't treat me as special. She didn't tell me anything, not about her home, or her family. It felt as if I was taking a great big leap into darkness. And, to be honest, I wasn't 100 per cent sure I could trust Gracie to hold my hand . . .

Dad was up on the stage. He was a good MC. His jokes made even Rosebud's face twitch into a grin. He was announcing something.

'No, no, no!' The howl of protest from the packed bodies around me startled me.

'What did he say?' I asked Grace.

'That stupid man,' said Gracie, tossing her head. 'He talk about a dance competition.'

I was as surprised as she was. 'But there isn't a dance competition tonight. Nobody's practised.'

Dad had decided, just out of the blue, to announce a dance competition. I knew what he was trying to do. He was trying to make up for the disappointment over the film. But it was a big mistake. He didn't understand that, didn't expect the outburst of anger from the floor. Mum, just back from flashing her torch in the bushes, looked bewildered too.

Typical of them, I was thinking. How long have they been here? More than twenty years. And what have they learned? Nothing.

It was embarrassing. I forgot how I'd looked in their window, and ached to go in for a hug. I felt more distance between us than ever.

Ruthlessly, as if I was seeing a stranger on the stage, I watched my dad mess things up even more.

'I will give £2,' he said, 'out of my own pocket, to the winners.' He held up the notes.

There was an outcry. Two pounds was serious money. Even the richest students only got £1 pocket money a term. To the poor ones, like Esther, that prize money was a fortune.

'It is not fair!' several people shouted. I shouted, 'It is not fair!' too.

'We have not practised!' yelled N'daka. 'We have not even chosen our partners!'

Up on the stage, Mum and Dad were having urgent discussions. They should have backed down, postponed the competition until the next school dance. But I knew what they were saying. They were saying, 'We can't back down. We mustn't give in to N'daka.' They thought backing down meant they'd lose their authority over us. They didn't know what I had known for ages now. That their authority was an illusion. It could be snuffed out as easily as a reed torch in the lake.

'I will start the music,' said Dad. 'And then we will eliminate the couples. When we, or Mr Lungu, touch you on the shoulder—'

'No, no, no.'

Angry chanting drowned him out. I was chanting too, louder than anyone. Mr Lungu, who taught us Geography, stood unhappily by the door.

'You must,' bawled Dad, 'sit down if you are touched on the shoulder!'

The music started. As if someone had jerked our strings we began to dance. My parents and Mr Lungu forced their way through, tapping shoulders, anyone's shoulder, just to thin out the crowd. But people left the floor without complaining. I was amazed. The dance competition seemed to be going smoothly after all. I noticed the relieved smile on Mum's face as she moved among the dancers. Mr Lungu shrugged, nervously, and eliminated me and Gracie. I started protesting but Gracie left the floor, good as gold, and pulled me after her.

'What are you going for? It's a joke! He should eliminate Chirwa and Lily before us. We're much better than them.'

But Gracie went, 'Shhhh.' She said, 'Wait.'

Another record started, to eliminate the few couples left dancing and find the winners. But everyone who'd been eliminated got up and danced so the floor was just as crowded as before.

Only I didn't know the plan. When they all moved like one person back onto the dance floor only I didn't know what was going on. Gracie had to drag me after her.

'Come on, girl.'

I hadn't seen any whispering. If people had whispered the plan to each other, they'd left me out. Did they think I'd betray them, tell Mum and Dad? I pushed that crazy idea right out of my head. No, I thought. They'd never think that. I just couldn't believe it. Everyone knew whose side I was on. Who stole Kellogg's cornflakes? Who pinched the record player for picnics? Who made fun of their own mum and dad in the dorm?

But, somehow, Gracie knew about the plan. She hauled me to my feet as soon as the second record started.

'But we're not in the competition—'

'Just keep dancing, girl,' she hissed in my ear.

Esther knew about it too. She was dancing next to us, with Reen. Esther's flip-flops, her only pair, were mended with my mum's hairgrips—the ones Esther had dived to collect during the food raid.

The competition was over. There could be no more elimination. Even my mum and dad realized that.

And now things were getting ugly. N'daka, always hot-tempered, was boiling over: 'We will not move!' he was yelling. 'We will go on strike! We will go on strike!'

My parents had lost control. We all knew it. Then the generator cut out. It was 9.30. No one lit the hurricane lamps.

I saw Mr Lungu slip away, probably to raise the alarm, to fetch some back-up.

I heard Mum's shrill voice, 'Girls, girls, we are going back to the dormitories. Follow me!'

Some girls obeyed her. I could see them grouping in the moonlight, by the door. But I couldn't get to them. Little David Itimu staggered into me. His head was thrown back and he was *yip, yip, yipping,* like a happy hyena, just to add to the din.

The hall was a dark furnace of steamy, struggling bodies. I was scared out of my wits. I couldn't see one friendly face. Grace had been whirled away from me in the crush.

'Get out of here, you *azungus!*' someone yelled. 'We do not want you here any more. Go back to your own country.'

They are shouting at Mum and Dad, I thought.

But I bolted too. Wild excited eyes flashed like wet pearls in the gloom. Grotesque shadows danced about on the walls. I fought my way to the door. Someone snatched at my hair. The red and yellow beads Esther had spent the afternoon threading on shot off and were trampled underfoot.

Now there were other voices. Mr Chilolo was there, the deputy headmaster, commanding the boys to go back to their dormitories.

'No, no, we are on strike. We will not move.'

Like a scowling Chief, N'daka was sitting on the stage, legs crossed, arms folded on his chest, glaring down at us all. His followers from his village, from his own tribe, were clustered round him, ready to die for him. 'Yes, we are on strike!'

'Girls, boys, think of St Mark's!' came Mum's reedy voice from somewhere near the door.

'Ha!' said someone, laughing right into my face.

A band of us girls set off in the pitch-black for our dormitories, clinging together, our only light my mum's torch. She didn't shine it on the path but swung it about, probing the bushes not for lovers but to scare off leopards or hyenas. Once Esther had been stalked by a leopard all the way up to the hill top. She had seen its green eyes glowing in the dark.

Lily's teeth were chattering with fear. Grace was at the back, dragging the stragglers along. Some, in their frantic efforts to keep up, threw away their dancing sandals. In the morning we found the sandals, dangling from tree branches, like gold and silver flowers.

I stumbled, trod on the back of a girl's flip-flop. 'Oh, sorry!' That was a bad thing to do, catch the heel of somebody's flip-flop. Flip-flops always fell apart when you did that. But tonight, nobody told me off.

There was crashing, whooping in the bushes as animals ran away from Mum's light.

Then we heard a noise behind us, someone running to catch up. It was Dad, his breath rasping, his chest heaving.

'Quick,' he said, 'get the girls back, barricade the doors. The boys are coming up here.'

So N'daka had changed his mind. He wasn't on strike. He was launching an attack on the girls' dormitories.

Mum had told me about another school, in another country, where some boys got drunk and broke into the girls' dormitories. Two girls were crushed to death under their iron bedsteads. They say one was raped.

I could hear my own voice whimpering in terror.

'Those boys are just playing silly games—' I started to say, thinking about little David Itimu, having the time of his life, playing at being a hyena.

'Come on!' Grace hauled me roughly by my long hair. 'You don't understand—N'daka is leading them. We must pile things against the door.'

I had never heard her so urgent, so desperate before. This wasn't the Gracie I knew. This Gracie scared and upset me.

We spent that night, all of us, crammed into one dormitory, trembling behind a barricade of iron bedsteads. Outside there was terror and confusion. Boys beat tin plates with sticks and shrieked defiance.

We saw fires, heard jeeps grinding up to the hill top. Once, we heard screaming in the night. Headlights swung crazily across the dormitory walls.

But no one tried to break in.

At last there was quiet. Some of us slept, in each other's arms to keep warm.

Gracie and I limped out, stiff and sore-eyed, into the first light of dawn. The mountains, over the border, were on fire with crimson light. The air smelled of burnt sugar. We learned later that a drunk boy had torched someone's maize garden, on his rampage up the track.

We learned also that only a few boys had come up the hill. Most had gone quietly back to their own dormitories. Even N'daka had been persuaded by Mr Chilolo to go. Only a handful, drunk with beer from the turn-off, had staggered up the hill. The jeeps we heard were police jeeps. Mr Jawali had called them. They took the drunk boys away.

N'daka was not punished. But Danny Nyong'onya was expelled, sent back to South Africa. None of us could believe it—we were sure a mistake had been made. But N'daka and some others swore that it was Danny at the front, mad with drink, urging on the attackers.

'That N'daka, he lies through his teeth,' hissed Grace.

Agnes, Danny's girlfriend, who was taking him steady, did not even have the chance to say goodbye. She got really depressed. Her heart was breaking. She didn't eat. She hid in bed for days with the blankets pulled up over her head. There was nothing we could do to make her feel better.

The morning after that terrible night, I joined Mum and Dad for breakfast on their *khonde* instead of eating maize porridge with my friends. I don't know why I did that—I just felt like some sugary tea and toast with marmalade to cheer me up.

The breakfast table was just the same as always—blue checked cloth, Ricory coffee. But my parents' faces were grey with tiredness and strain.

Dad tried to cheer Mum up: 'There was no harm done. It's not so dreadful. Some boys got out of hand, got a little bit drunk. Just high spirits really. It's all over now.'

But Mum couldn't be comforted. She was really upset. She thought it was personal—that the pupils had let her down. 'I can't believe it could happen here at St Mark's,' she said. 'What if they close us down? Remember that high school up north, Chola, Cholu, what on earth was it called?'

'Come on,' said Dad. 'It's not that bad. We're not some unimportant little school up north. *Government Ministers* send their children here. There'd be an outcry if St Mark's was closed.'

They didn't close us down. Mum said we were lucky. That it had all been hushed up. But me and the girls all thought like my dad—that they would never close down St Mark's. We were the best.

Except that, two days later, a black limousine appeared and took away Edith, the Minister for Public Works's daughter. And Rosebud, the Minister for Agriculture's daughter, went home for the weekend and never came back. Neither of them were popular, so me and my friends didn't worry about it, at the time.

Everything seemed to settle down. It was the old St Mark's routine—breakfast, flag raising, lessons, lunch, games, supper, private study, lights out. Every day more or less the same.

The two main things in my head were going to Grace's and my studies. We were all serious students. We wanted to do well in our exams. If she passed her exams, Esther could escape from her village and get work in the capital, in some government department. I never found out what Grace wanted to do when she passed her exams. She never talked about it.

Then, suddenly, we went to flag raising one morning and Lovemore wasn't there. He'd just disappeared. That didn't surprise us much—he'd always been a joke. Nobody seemed to know where he'd gone. Mama Jelenje had disappeared too. Gary said Lovemore had probably been banished to some primary school in the backwoods, where they still taught the kids under mango trees.

Lovemore's replacement was tougher, uglier, and yelled a lot louder. But even he couldn't make us march in step.

PART THREE

M'LINDI

SEVEN

Grace and I were alone on the outskirts of town, waiting for a bus.

At last term was over—it was nearly Christmas—and I was going to her village, to meet her family.

It was really happening. 'Are you certain this visit is still on?' Mum kept asking me, as the end of term drew closer. I wasn't certain. But Gracie had never said it was off. And I daren't ask her directly in case she denied ever inviting me.

During the busy routine of the school day we scarcely spoke. And at night, in the dormitory, there was never any privacy. There was no more time alone, like at Zinja, or at the swimming hole. But I kept the faith, still yearning for the time when we'd be inseparable.

I imagined us in her village, linked arm in arm, cooled by the shade of a lemon tree, exchanging secrets, like sisters.

So it didn't matter that she didn't speak to me in school. In her village it would all be different. I carried that thought in my mind, as a beggar child holds a precious shilling in her hand and every few seconds opens her fingers to look at it.

And, as we waited at the bus stop, what I hoped for seemed to be coming true. Grace was really nice to me, all her spikiness turned to honey.

'You will have nice days in my village,' she said. 'You can meet my relatives. We will go to meet my friends on the football field.'

It struck me again, with a tiny flutter of fear in my stomach, how little I knew about her or where I was going. It was a village close to the border, with tea

69

plantations all around it. Her mum ran a general store while her dad worked in the city and only came home at weekends. That's all I knew.

'So how many brothers and sisters do you have?' I'd asked her.

'Oh, I cannot count them!' she said.

I was interested in her family (I was interested in everything about her) but every time I asked about them, she closed up, like a porcupine.

I'd tried to tell Mum. I said, 'This visit to Grace's— it's all a bit vague. I don't know hardly anything about her family.' But Mum seemed preoccupied these days. She just said, 'Oh, Grace will look after you. I'm not worried at all.'

The bus was already an hour late.

I'd never been to town without my parents. I'd never been to this part of town at all. Maybe we'd passed through it in the VW. Stupidly, I looked around for a glimpse of metallic blue, even though I knew my dad's car couldn't be here. He was miles away, up at the swimming hole, still trying to snap pythons. Augustus had told him there were two up there now, making love, writhing together like those twisted candy sticks you get at Mr Khan's store.

'Are you certain this is the bus stop?' I'd asked Grace when she dumped her suitcase.

'Sure,' she'd shrugged.

The town was behind us. In front of us the road stretched into the distance and dissolved in the heat haze. It was eerily empty. No children, no lorries, not even a wandering chicken or goat, even though there was a jumble of shacks along it. Then I adjusted my eyes, saw that there were people, swarms of them, watching us from the darkness of doorways, from the shadows under the trees.

'What is this place?' I asked, drawing closer to Gracie.

'It is the bus stop!'

But there was nothing to show it was a bus stop. No sign or mark on the road. Nobody else was waiting.

'Why are those people staring?'

'Because you are white, of course. They do not see many *azungus* in this part of town. And also they are staring because I look so fine in my new dress.'

She did look fine. I was proud to be with her. She was like a princess. I shuffled my flip-flops, couldn't meet all those watchers' eyes. But Grace tilted her chin up defiantly, as if to say, 'Watch all you like. Feast your eyes. What do I care?'

For the first time I thought what a strange couple we made. Her skin coppery, mine pasty. I was small—she was tall and elegant. I had big flat feet that slapped down when I walked. Gracie had a light, springy step. No wonder they were staring. Also, Gracie already looked like a woman. I looked like a skinny girl, young for my age. I had no hips to sway when dancing, no breasts to fill my bra. Mum had told me, 'Don't worry, white girls develop late in Africa.' I had started my periods just a few months before. And the only sanitary towels Mr Khan sold were horrible—big and bulky like nappies. They gave you heat rash.

I never knew what day my periods would start. There was no warning, apart from some stomach cramps. I stood at the bus stop worrying that I might start in the night at Grace's house and wake up to find red stains on her mum's sheets.

I'd die then, I was thinking. I'd just die.

I wondered whether I ought to wear towels all the time (I had four packets of them in my suitcase) just to be safe.

The bus didn't come. There was still a forest of gleaming eyes in the shadows. I couldn't find my way back from here to the main part of town. We'd come through a vast estate of grey concrete huts with tin roofs. They all looked like tiny boxes. There were streets and streets of them. The streets had no names, just numbers. And suddenly I was chilled by dread. Even my sweat felt freezing cold, although the sun was hammering down on our heads.

I thought wild thoughts: Maybe the bus isn't coming. Maybe Grace is going to run away and leave me here.

'It is here,' said Grace, squinting into the distance. 'And not so late as it usually is. This is a very good start to our journey. You will like my village, Trish. We will have good holidays there.'

I picked up my suitcase, heaved it closer to the road. Relief bathed me like a shower. The bus had arrived.

Grace was so chatty, so charming and friendly. It was going to be great. I got excited all over again. I felt ashamed of what I'd just thought—about Gracie abandoning me. I told myself off: 'Don't be so stupid. She wouldn't have left you here, all on your own.'

EIGHT

The bus crawled up country, its windows sealed with dust so you couldn't see out. But I knew we were crossing that plain I looked down on every morning from the hill top at St Mark's.

I imagined Dad sitting on the *khonde*, like an all-seeing wizard, checking my progress through his telephoto lens. It was a stupid idea. I knew he couldn't see this far. But I liked to think he could, all the same.

The bus was heaving with people—chickens squawking in baskets, babies sticky with milk crawling about under seats. There were bicycles strapped to the roof, bananas bouncing around in the luggage racks. And the aisle was so full of boxes, baskets, suitcases, that, even if I'd changed my mind about going to Grace's, I could never have fought my way off.

I wasn't sitting with Grace. She was further down the bus. I was wedged in beside a fat mama who spread her knees wide and made a hammock of her skirt to hold her dinner. Her dinner was *nsima* in a tin cooking pot. She scooped out the white porridge, shaped it into a ball with her fingers, tossed it into her mouth.

'Eat!' she said to me, shoving the pot towards me. 'Eat!'

I took a handful, just to be polite. When I thanked her she said '*Aieee!*' and opened her eyes very wide. She was amazed that I spoke her language. I thought, What's so amazing about that? I was born here, wasn't I? This is my home too.

Sometimes I could see Grace through the squash of people. Her hair was done in the holiday style, plaited round her head like the spiral of a shell. I could hear her laugh, rich and deep. She was chatting with the person next to her. I craned my neck, jealously, for a better view. But I couldn't see who she was talking to.

The bus rocked on for hours and hours. I dozed, my head nodding. The mama ate groundnuts and mangoes and chewed some sugarcane.

A sudden rainstorm rattled on the roof. It woke me up and gave me a streaky view from the bus windows. All I could see were tea fields, miles and miles of them, with women moving among the rows, picking tea.

Then suddenly, like the most spectacular show on earth, a mountain slid into view. Just one towering mountain rising from the plain like a giant's castle. Except its craggy sides were green with forests and a hundred waterfalls ran glistening down like silver threads. It was incredible—magical, mysterious. It took my breath away.

The top of it was hidden by delicate pink mists that looped it, like the rings round Saturn.

'What is that mountain?' I asked the mama.

She peered through the window, shrugged and said, 'That? That is Mount M'lindi.'

'*Ahh!*' I knew something about M'lindi. I had learned it in geography at St Mark's. It was a very weird place. There were primeval forests on that mountain, hung with mosses. And the kind of ferns and plants that dinosaurs used to graze upon . . .

'We are here,' said Grace bluntly as the bus jolted to a stop.

She had fought her way back up the aisle and was squashing aside the mama's bust, like two big, plumped-up pillows, so she could drag me out from my seat.

'*Aiee,*' objected the mama as I wrestled my suitcase out of the luggage rack. A mango plopped into her cooking pot. She fished it out and took a bite.

'*Cha!*' She threw it on the floor in disgust—it wasn't ripe yet.

'Sorry, sorry, sorry,' I said, as I pushed past her.

Grace had disappeared. Suddenly, desperate that I might get left behind, I charged down the bus.

'Sorry, sorry . . . '

I tripped over a basket of charcoal, sent it clinking along the aisle. The metal corners of my suitcase jabbed someone's legs.

'Sorry!'

'So here you are at last,' said Grace when I fell out of the bus.

With crashing gears, the bus shuddered off in a cloud of yellow dust.

We were alone, me and Gracie, on a dirt road, with some buildings in the distance. Mount M'lindi was over to the north. It was late afternoon. The hoops of mist round the top were changing from pink to deep purple.

I got my first view of Grace's village as, hunched over like Quasimodo, I hauled my suitcase through it. All those sanitary towels made it feel as if it weighed a ton.

'Come on, girl.' Grace walked eagerly in front of me, with her suitcase balanced on her head. I'd never been able to carry things like that, though I'd almost broken my neck trying.

It was a one-street village—Indian shops, verandahs, tin roofs. Everything dusty and bleached nearly white by the sun. There was no one about, as if it was a ghost town.

The long bus ride had made me hot, itchy, queasy. I kept dropping my suitcase, squeezing my hand to get the blood pumping again into my grey, dead fingers. I felt odd, dazed, a bit unreal.

'Here is our shop,' said Grace. 'And here is Mum, waiting to welcome you.'

Grace's mum had a green dress on—she was short and squat. I thought, Grace must take after her dad.

Grace's mum was holding a baby boy in her arms. He was about six months old. The baby had a string of blue glass beads round his neck. He was cramming a passion fruit into his mouth—the pink juice trickling down his chin.

'Hello!' I gave Grace's mum my best smile. I wanted her to like me. I wanted all of Grace's family to like me.

The baby cringed back and hid his face in Grace's mum's dress.

'He is shy,' I said. I leaned forward. I was going to gurgle at him, say how fat he was, how healthy, so that Grace's mum would be pleased.

Then the baby poked his face out and stared at me again. His shocked brown eyes were wide as pennies.

'Hello!' I tickled him under his fat, sticky chin. 'I know who you are. You are Heston. You're Grace's little brother.'

He let out an ear-splitting wail: '*Waaaaa!*' He kicked his little fat legs in distress. His chubby fingers clenched at the cotton dress.

Dismayed, I backed off. 'I don't think he likes me,' I said in English.

But Grace's mum didn't speak English. She nodded at me, and smiled, as if there wasn't a terrified child kicking and howling in her arms.

I was horribly embarrassed. 'What did I do? What did I do wrong?'

Grace laughed. 'He is scared. He has never seen an *azungu* before. He probably thinks you are the white devil come from the lake to get him. We tell our children that story if they don't behave. We say a fish devil will crawl out from the lake at night. And she is all white, just like you. White all over and slimy, like a fish's belly, like a corpse. And she will snatch you from your bed and drag you down to her home at the bottom of the lake, like crocodiles do. And you will be stuck there, in the mud. And you will never see your mummy and daddy no more.'

'Is that the white witch you told me and Esther about—the one with the long nails? No wonder he's scared . . . '

'No, this one is different—she does not have long nails. But she is just as scary.'

Oh, great, I thought, miserably. That's just great.

'My little sisters will be scared of you too,' laughed Gracie as if it was a big joke.

'So every kid in the village is going to be scared of me, are they? They'll all be wetting their pants, soon as I come near? They'll all think I'm this fish-devil thing from the lake?'

I was horrified. I wanted them to think I was a nice person. 'What am I supposed to do, go round with a bag over my head?'

Grace grinned at my frantic, whispered questions. Just at that moment a straggle of little kids came past. I steeled myself for more howling. But they were only curious. They walked backwards staring; they didn't run away. They didn't seem to have heard the story of the white fish-devil-woman from the lake.

Hovering around behind Gracie's mum was an old bloke. He looked distinguished, with grey hair and a beard. Anxious to make up for scaring Heston, I sprang towards the old man, grasped his hand and shook it. His hand felt as thin and papery as onion skin.

'Hello,' I told him. 'I'm Gracie's friend. Thank you for inviting me to your house.'

He mumbled something, dropped my hand and shuffled off into the shop. Then I saw that he wore tatty shorts and car tyre flip-flops, mended with wire.

Grace shouted with laughter. 'That is not my dad. My

dad is working in the city. He is only home at weekends. That is our servant, Ezekiel!'

She explained my mistake to her mum—who giggled politely behind her hand.

They sat me on a chair in the best parlour. It was very lush. The wooden floor was stained red as betel juice. Red cloths with red fringes draped all the furniture. Gracie vanished into the kitchen to help her mum prepare the meal. I could hear them laughing and talking. Little girls came to peep at me, then ran away, giggling.

At last dinner was ready. We had rice with omelettes on top cut into strips and a cabbage and fish stew. Gracie's mum pushed the fish stew towards me and smiled and made eating motions with her hands, 'Eat! Eat!' The little girls rocked with laughter. The table was crowded.

'Who are all these people?' I whispered when Grace came in from the kitchen with a pile of plates.

'Oh, they are my four little sisters and my big brother who works in the shop. His name is Peter.'

I knew then that there would be no more privacy here than at St Mark's. And Gracie would need my company even less. Why had I kidded myself there would be just the two of us? Gracie seemed more out of reach than ever.

I was dizzy with tiredness and lonely and homesick. Suddenly I wanted desperately to go home to St Mark's. But I was stuck here, among strangers—even Gracie seemed like a stranger—with no way of contacting my mum and dad and no idea when I could catch the next bus back to town.

I smiled and smiled at everyone until my jaw ached.

There were red cockroaches in the tin toilet bowl, waving hairy feelers at me. That didn't bother me much. Our chim at home had cockroaches. Only ours were orange. What really bothered me was that Grace's chim, out in their back yard, was in a wooden hut. There were spaces between the planks to let in fresh air. I squatted above the chim, out of reach of those feelers, listening for giggles, in case those little sisters were out there, spying on me. At least I hadn't started a period yet . . .

That night, I shared a bedroom with Grace's sisters. Grace had deserted me again. It was her mum who, smiling all the time, shooed me into the bedroom as if she was shooing chickens, and her big brother Peter who dumped my suitcase on an iron cot.

It was a bitter blow. I couldn't believe it—I was hideously disappointed. I felt hot tears prickling under my eyelids. I'd taken it for granted that Gracie and me would be sharing a bedroom. That we could talk to each other, privately, maybe far into the night. And that would make up for everything.

But there was a double bed next to my iron cot. Grace's four little sisters were already sitting there, in a row, swinging their twiggy legs. And staring at me with unblinking eyes.

They had home-made white frocks on, with their hair scraped up and frizzed out into enormous pom-poms, twice as big as their heads.

They looked excited, as if they were waiting for something.

I thought, What am I supposed to do now?

Then I realized. They were waiting for me to take my clothes off. It was a sure bet that they hadn't seen an *azungu* naked before.

I flapped my hands at them, 'Go away. I want to get undressed.'

I was so weary, so worn out with travelling and with the strain of smiling that all I wanted to do was sleep.

But the sisters just laughed, then nudged each other

into silence. They stared at me, narrowing their eyes, concentrating hard, like I was a difficult sum in Maths.

So what? I thought. I was just too tired to care. And they were only kids. I slipped my dress off over my head.

'Eeeeee!' The little sisters gave a long, long sigh of satisfaction. They nudged each other some more. Then they settled down again, like the audience at a show, to watch.

It broke my nerve.

I was wearing one of Mr Khan's roomy white bras. The cups looked like collapsed balloons. They were for big mamas really, with breasts like cushions, not for girls with no bust like me. And I was wearing another thing from Mr Khan's shop. He'd just got a shipment of stretchy, elastic knickers called panty girdles. They made your stomach flat. They made you sweat as well. It felt like you were in the greasy grip of a python. But Mr Khan told us they were the latest thing from UK. He said all UK girls wore them. So we all rushed to buy one, even the skinniest, with stomachs as flat as chapattis.

I couldn't do it. I couldn't take off any more clothes under those greedy eyes.

I pulled my cotton nightdress over my head with my bra still on. Then, fumbling under it, I tried to wriggle out of my new panty girdle. I don't know how UK girls do it but it's very hard work. I managed to force it down over my hips. Then I let it slither to my ankles in a wrinkly white tube.

'Aieeeee!'

One of the little girls gave a shriek of pure horror. Her hand flew to her mouth. Another's mouth stretched to a big, round O. She was trying to scream but no scream would come out.

They bolted, the whole gang of them. There was a

tangle of arms and legs in the doorway as they all tried to force their way out at once. Then, they burst through and took off like hares. I could hear them shrieking, hear their flip-flops slapping somewhere on a hard, mud floor.

I stood there, frozen, my panty girdle still round my ankles, staring after them. Ages seemed to pass. The house had suddenly gone very quiet.

Then Gracie came in.

'What did I do?' I begged her. 'Why did they run away?'

Gracie laughed at the bewilderment on my face.

'Those ignorant kids. They told me you took off your clothes. And then you took your white skin off. Like a snake they said. "That *azungu* is peeling off her skin like a snake!"' Grace mimicked their shrill, terrified voices.

'Did you tell them? Did you tell them it was just my panty girdle?' I picked up the crinkled roll of elastic and shoved it out of sight under my pillow. 'Did you tell them what it was?'

'No, I tell them you remove all your skin. That you are sitting on your bed now, just a skeleton. I tell them white people do that every night, take their skin off, hang it up to get the creases out, like we hang up our clothes, and then they climb back into it in the morning.'

Grace threw her head back and whooped with laughter, delighted with her joke.

'I'll never make friends with them now. Why do you say things like that?'

Grace shrugged, 'Because they are just uneducated kids.'

I flung myself onto the bed. 'Now your baby brother thinks I'm a white fish devil woman and your sisters think I take my skin off at night. I wanted them all to like me. Why did you tell them those things?'

I felt very sorry for myself, all alone, far from home, at the mercy of such cruelty.

Then with shocking suddenness, I felt myself break down. Tears came crashing through like breakers. I cried and cried, in great, heaving sobs, wailing as loud as Heston.

'It isn't fair! It isn't fair!' I sobbed.

I stopped eventually. The sound of my own crying embarrassed me. I gulped back tears, sniffed and smeared my hot face with the hem of my nightie.

Grace smiled at me, a brilliant smile. She sat down on the bed beside me. It was the first time we had ever been alone in a room together.

I sniffed some more. I was trembling, red-eyed, hiccuping from my crying fit. 'I'm just tired, Gracie,' I told her, rubbing at my eyes. 'I'm just so tired.'

'*Cha*,' said Grace, her voice gentle and full of kindness. 'I forgot. I shouldn't tease you. You are still a baby yet, aren't you?'

She had scented oil on her hair, making it glossy. She smelled of mimosa flowers.

She stuck out her own lip, mimicking my glum face. 'I guess that you are real mad with me now,' she said.

I shook my head, dumbly.

'Tomorrow,' she said, 'you will feel better. It is just because it is strange here. Everything is strange.'

As she spoke, she was plaiting my damp hair the way she sometimes used to do on school dance night in our dormitory.

'It still won't plait,' I told her with a watery grin. 'It's too fine.'

But she didn't stop. I grew calmer as she plaited my hair, as if I was a nervous dog being stroked. I thought how childish, how silly I'd been. 'Nothing bad is going to happen here,' I told myself. 'Nothing bad is going to happen.'

'And anyway,' said Grace, 'you take things too serious, Trish. You have no need to be mad with me. I did not really tell my sisters that thing I told you—about *azungus* hanging up their skin.'

NINE

Next morning, they sat me on a chair in the shop. The shop was a general store—it sold everything from hoes, fertilizers, sacks of maize, to golden dancing sandals and Ambi skin lightening lotion. Peter rushed around the shop, doing his chores. He didn't smile at me, or even look at me.

I could see through an open door into the house. I saw Ezekiel, with a sweeping brush made of thorn twigs, cross from room to room. I saw Grace's mum with Heston strapped on her back, hurrying from the kitchen to the yard calling chickens, *'Choo, choo, choo!'*

A little sister came to peep at me—I smiled but she dashed away. Otherwise, no one paid me any attention. Even the customers in the shop gave me one stare, then forgot me. I felt as if I was invisible.

There was no sign of Grace. She hadn't been at breakfast—I hadn't seen her since she plaited my hair last night.

I didn't want to get in anyone's way, they were busy people. So I just sat there.

I looked down at my big, white feet, hugging the floor like flatfish. I watched a shiny blue fly batting itself against the window.

At St Mark's, no one ever sat still this long, doing nothing. There were always bells, dinner gongs, driving you on through the tightly-packed day.

Time dragged until I had no idea what time it was.

The shop cat did a twirling leap and snatched the blue fly out of the air. I could hear the fly buzzing, trapped inside the cat's mouth. Then the cat gulped it down.

The shop door was open. I could see Mount M'lindi.

84

The waterfalls reflected the sun. It was dazzling, blinding, like a white fireball. I stared at it. I think I was getting light-headed, hallucinating, with all that sitting in one place. The mountain seemed to grow smaller, then larger, then smaller, pumping in and out like a beating heart . . .

Then, when I was nearly crazy with boredom and sitting still, Grace came in, wearing her blue and scarlet *zambia*, the one she wore at Zinja. She spoke to me, 'Did you sleep well?' My mind stopped drifting. I stopped feeling invisible. I felt real again.

'I have been asleep all this while,' said Grace, yawning.

'Look,' I said. 'Can't I help? I mean, everyone is so busy. Can't I help anyone?'

'You are an honoured guest!' laughed Gracie. 'Guests do not work.'

She didn't apologize for leaving me on my own all this time. Grace never made excuses, never apologized. I always wished I had that kind of style.

Things looked instantly brighter now Gracie was here. She yawned a bit more, stretched, came awake and when she did she was friendly, lively, confidential—in one of her best, most sparkling moods. I immediately forgave her for neglecting me.

'*Cha*, that Peter,' she said, when her brother went out of the shop. 'He works, works, works. He is a boring fellow. He does not smile. And he is uneducated. He didn't even get his Primary Leaving Certificate.'

She gave me strong orange tea in a metal mug. She said, 'My mum will be mad I have not given you the best cups.'

We sat alone, giggling in the kitchen, eating bread spread with margarine from a tin. It was great. I thought: This is more like it. This is how I thought it would be.

'We will go out together,' said Grace. 'I will show you my home town.'

She left me again. Not for so long this time. She came back dressed up. She had a glittery dress on—I'd never seen it before. It was red with a deep gold hem. Her hair was glossy with mimosa oil. She wore a necklace, of red glass beads. I didn't know she had clothes this fine. I thought she had put them on in honour of my visit. And to swank about the town, showing off to her friends.

I didn't want to show her up. 'Shall I change my dress?' I asked her. 'I've got my best dress, in my suitcase.'

She looked puzzled. 'There is no need for you to do that,' she said.

So we went out into the bright, hot day to parade before the town. I felt like an ugly duckling beside her, a gawky little girl in my sensible, faded cotton print frock. But nothing could spoil the thrill of being with her. Just the two of us together, walking arm in arm as if we'd been best friends for the whole of our lives.

Gracie showed me the football field. It was like every football field I'd ever seen, yellow and shrivelled. She showed me the primary school.

She said: 'I went to that primary school. Our teacher there was called Miss Ulili.'

We walked past the new water tower. Then Grace said, 'I have shown you my village. There is nothing else to see.'

But instead of going home, Grace went into the Indian shop behind us. I stayed on the verandah, not knowing if I was supposed to follow her inside. Minutes passed. Then she came out of the dark cave of the shop and beckoned me inside.

'Why you waiting out there, girl?' she said. 'Come on in.'

Bales of cloth were stacked on the shelves. Some of it plain cotton, like my dresses. Some of it, on the highest shelves, was gorgeous gold and silver, for wedding saris.

A woman was perched behind the counter in a blue sari.

It was difficult to see her in the gloom. Gold bangles clinked on her plump arms. She had a thin, beaky nose that made her face look hawk-like. But her smile was kind. She didn't look surprised to see me. It was as if I was expected. She held her hand palm upwards in greeting, then waved us towards the back of the shop. Grace didn't introduce me to her.

'Where we going?' I whispered to Gracie.

'You will see.'

I followed her into a room behind the shop. It was stuffy and dim. A fan was clunking round above our heads. But it hardly disturbed the hot air.

'Sit here,' said Grace.

I sat, on an orange plastic settee. People with money lived here. The floor was varnished glossy red. There was cloth everywhere, hung with heavy gold fringes and fat silver tassels. The windows were barred. There were many possessions—a radio, a sewing machine, and on a table by the sofa, a record player.

'Where is this place?' I whispered. 'Do you have friends here, Gracie?'

But Grace wasn't listening to me. She had eyes only for the boy who came in through a beaded curtain that led to another room.

'This is Levi,' said Grace. I think she was talking to me although she never took her eyes off him.

Levi was about eighteen. He was very handsome, with full lips and a hawk nose. The smell of sweet oil came into the room with him—it was on his hair, to keep it shiny and slicked back. I didn't like him.

'We will not be long,' said Grace briskly. 'You do not move. You sit here.'

Levi walked over to the settee. He was wearing a snow-white tunic, baggy trousers and sandals. He was not pure Indian, but Indian and African mixed.

'Oh, pardon,' he said, as he reached past me to switch on the record player.

Grace giggled, her eyes darting nervously towards the shop where Levi's mummy was.

'We must hurry,' she told him.

Grace snatched red beads from round her neck. The necklace spilled into my hand.

'Hold these for two seconds,' she said.

The music twanged, the singer wailed in my ear. Levi came back and turned it up, louder.

Then they disappeared into the other room. And I saw, before they let the bead curtain fall, that it was a bedroom. And the bed had a white quilt on it.

But I still wouldn't let myself believe it. 'They are old school chums,' a prim voice in my head told me. 'They probably went to Primary together. They are probably talking about old times.'

I sat there, with the fan chuk-chukking above my head and the music jangling. My dress was sticking to the orange plastic. Grace's red bead necklace was dribbling through my fingers. I made my hand clench, to stop it, before it fell onto the floor and broke.

The record finished. In a flurry of clicking the arm jerked back to the beginning and it started all over again. Ages seemed to pass.

I sat there, my face flushed, Grace's red beads gripped in my hand, realizing that I had been set up.

'She is already a woman,' I told myself, savagely. 'Not an ignorant little girl like you are! Did you really think there was no boy who had the hots for her back home? Did you really think she invited you here because she wanted you for her best friend?'

Mummy was guarding the shop. She wasn't suspicious. She thought they were entertaining the *azungu* guest, feeding her tea and sticky sweets. She wouldn't leave the shop in case of thieves. She thought Levi and Grace were behaving themselves. They'd fixed her good. Just like they'd fixed me.

I sat there, wriggling on the sticky plastic seat, hating myself for my own naivety. I knew now that Gracie had no use for silly, immature girls. If she told secrets, they would be to Levi. If she needed company, it would be his. He was more important to her than I could ever be.

I didn't blame Gracie. I blamed myself. I felt hopeless, resigned. I should have expected this all along. I'd been an absolute fool not to see it coming.

The bead curtain rattled. I sprang to attention, like a sentry caught sleeping on duty.

Grace strolled in. Her silver sandals weren't on her feet any more. They were dangling from her fingers. She took her beads out of my hand and, without a word, fastened them back round her neck.

She didn't explain anything to me. Why should she?

Levi was worried about Mummy. He said, 'She will wonder where we are,' as Gracie slipped her sandals back on.

We all trooped back into the shop. Mummy didn't smell a rat. She thought an *azungu* guest was the perfect chaperone. She was eating slices of fried cassava, sprinkling one slice with salt, the next with lime. She gave me one to try. 'Eat, eat!' she said. 'Very good!' I took one, just to be polite. It tasted like sawdust in my mouth. I forced a smile on my face. 'Very good!' I said back. I wouldn't have told her what Levi and Grace had been up to, not in a million years.

'He is my boyfriend. I am taking him steady. We are going to be married when I pass my exams. Our families agree,' was what Gracie told me on our way back to her house. 'I am a lucky girl. He is one sweet guy, isn't he?'

'Oh yes,' I agreed with her. 'He is one sweet guy.'

We went round to Levi's house the next day. I sat there numbly. It was the same—the clunking fan, the gluey seat, the record player turned up loud. Only this time Mummy was dipping her cassava fries in chilli chutney. And Mount M'lindi, when we came out in late afternoon, was wrapped in mysterious blue shadow.

On my third day in Grace's village, after breakfast, I was sitting on my wooden chair in the shop. Ezekiel was sweeping the verandah. Peter was humping in sacks of maize from a truck parked outside. I didn't know where anyone else was—not Grace, or her four little sisters or her baby brother Heston, or her mum. The house seemed empty and echoing. As if everyone was somewhere else.

I sat gazing down at my cotton print dress, my white flatfish feet. A fly, a shiny green one this time, buzzed in the window. Soon, I would be taken to another house, sat on another chair, while Levi and Gracie . . .

And suddenly, I cracked. I couldn't stand it a moment longer. Sitting still was unbearable. It was driving me crazy. My legs started twitching, my hands shaking. I leapt up, sending the chair flying. I was trembling with outrage.

Where is that Gracie? I was thinking. How can she treat me like this!

'Where's Gracie?' I demanded.

'She is busy,' said Peter, looking curiously at me.

'Well, I will find her.'

I went rampaging through the house, looking for Grace. I was frantic, wild, desperate. I wanted to go home, back to St Mark's, *now*, this second. I couldn't stay here. I didn't belong here. I should never have come. It was all a terrible mistake.

The last bead curtain I yanked aside showed me Gracie, crouching on a stool, with baby Heston wriggling in her lap. He was feeding from her breast.

Gracie looked up as I crashed into the room.

'It is no good,' she said. 'My milk is all dried up.'

90

I couldn't speak. My head reeled, I had to lean against the wall.

'He is getting too old to suck anyway,' said Grace, pulling her *zambia* up over her breast. 'You have sharp teeth,' she said tenderly to Heston. 'You can eat banana, *nsima*, anything you want.'

I found my voice at last. But it didn't sound like my voice; it was high and broken. 'Why . . . why are you trying to breast feed your baby brother?' I asked her, appalled.

'He is not my brother, he is my son,' said Grace. 'N'daka is his dad.'

What she'd said was quite clear. But I couldn't seem to understand it. It was as if a black hole had opened up in my mind.

Grace saw the bewildered look on my face. 'Poor Trish,' she said. 'Sit down now you are here.'

I stumbled over to her bed, the room spinning round me.

The baby chewed on Grace's knuckles. 'I will take him to my mum soon,' said Gracie. 'She still has milk to give him, left over from my last little sister.'

'But you hate N'daka—'

'I do hate him,' Gracie agreed, nodding. 'I will hate him for ever.'

'Then why . . . ' I gestured helplessly at N'daka's son.

'Because he forced me. Last year, at school.'

'At St Mark's?'

I still had trouble making sense of what she was telling me. It kept trying to jumble itself in my head. I thought of my mum, probing the bushes with her torch for kissing couples, her ears flapping for the sound of tell-tale giggling in the dark. And I said a really stupid thing, 'But how could it happen? Was my mum on duty?'

'It was not after a school dance. Not in the dark. It

was in the broad day, behind the tuck shop, while Lovemore was raising the flag.'

'During the flag raising?'

'I said so!' snapped Grace.

Then she seemed to regret her anger because she said, quietly, 'He is very strong. He put his hand over my mouth. I almost died of choking. Afterwards I was sick on my school blouse . . . '

I couldn't control my face—it was twisting with distress and horror. 'N'daka! He is disgusting! I would like to kill him!'

But I hardly had time to warm to Gracie's shaky smile of gratitude before what I said next wiped it off her face. 'You should have told my mother,' I said.

'*Cha!*' Gracie spat out her scorn. Heston started to whimper. A rush of bitter words poured out of Gracie's mouth: 'Your mum, she see me in the afternoon after he had done what he did and she say, "Oh Grace, what is the matter with you, why is your face so sulky, you seem as if you have lost a shilling and found sixpence". And I tell her I have a headache so she give me two Aspirin! And, in any case, if I had told her it was during flag raising she would say, "Oh, Grace, you know what is the regulations! All students must attend at flag raising! That is a very strict rule!"'

'But N'daka must be punished—'

'Get real, girl. I would be the one getting punished! What could they do to N'daka. Eh? Eh? He is the headmaster's friend, his family is too powerful!'

Her whole body heaved with emotion. She was clutching at her throat, as if she couldn't breathe. I sat staring at her. I didn't know what to say, how to comfort her. I was so far out of my depth I was drowning.

Heston started screaming, plucking at her *zambia*. Gracie dragged a hand down over her tear-streaked face.

Then she said, in a flat, weary voice, 'I will take Heston to his grandma now.'

She let the curtain fall behind her. The baby's screams grew distant. I didn't know if she was coming back. But I sat there, on her bed. I didn't seem to have the strength to get up. I put my face in my hands, rocked myself to and fro, to and fro, trying to cool my boiling brain. It felt like the world I knew, or *thought* I knew, was collapsing in on me.

She did come back. She sat on the bed beside me. And the first thing she said was, 'You must tell no one. No one, Trish. It is a secret about Heston.'

Gracie was sharing secrets with me, something I had always longed for. But this was a secret I didn't want to hear about. I just wanted it to go away.

I asked her, 'So N'daka doesn't know?'

'No. And he will never know about Heston. His family will try to steal him away. And if I make trouble for N'daka at the school his people there will kill me.'

'You are joking, what, at St Mark's?'

I said this in amazement. I couldn't help it—as if St Mark's rules would protect her against the assassin's machete.

'You do not see anything, girl. Your mum and *gudji-gudji* they do not see anything. What is right in front of their eyes!'

I blushed. I felt naive, stupid again. I thought I'd known what was going on, been at the centre of things at school. But I never heard a whisper about the rape, never suspected that Gracie was pregnant, although I had seen her every day.

Grace was saying, 'N'daka has many of his tribe at St Mark's. And his family are big friends of the President . . . '

But I wanted to ask her about another thing. Politics didn't interest me—my world was the school and the intrigues of our dormitory. 'When you were pregnant, with your belly swelling, how did you keep it secret from the girls?'

Grace shrugged, as if that was easy. 'Those big school skirts, they hide everything. You remember Martha Masulu last year? She was pregnant. We used to laugh,' said Grace bitterly. 'She was sick every morning in the bushes on the way down to school. And still your mum did not guess . . . Anyway, my mum and me, we went away to an auntie in the north. We stayed two months, in the long holiday. I had Heston up there, in the north, and people here think he is my brother.'

I felt that I was far, far out at sea. I couldn't cope with this.

'But . . . but what about Levi?' I asked Grace.

'That is why Heston must be a secret. I am betrothed to Levi. We will marry after I take my exams. His mummy is thinking I am still a virgin. And she does not really like my colour but she will allow the marriage because my family has a shop, we are quite rich—and she and my mum are in Mothers' Union together. But she does not know about Heston. Even Levi does not know. So you must never tell. Promise! You must promise, Trish.'

'I promise.' At last there was one thing I could do for Gracie. I could keep her secret. I knew I would die rather than tell it.

'I hate that N'daka!' I told her again.

'Yes.' But she said it with a sort of cold despair in her eyes.

'And when Heston was first born,' she told me, 'I hated *him* too. For a long time I could not hold him . . . But one day,' and here she spoke with that old fire that made me hope that, maybe, her spirit wasn't broken, 'one day I will scratch his father's eyes out. I will kill him, if I get the chance.'

94

I sat on her bed, my mind heavy as clay, loaded down with what I'd learned. I was ashamed that last term, when she didn't talk to me enough, didn't pay me enough attention, I'd known nothing about her pain. I'd only thought of my own.

Then a terrible suspicion bubbled up through the confusion in my brain. I didn't want to ask her. I had to.

'Did Esther know—that you were pregnant? Did the other girls in our dormitory know?'

'Yes, some knew. But they are sworn to secrecy. They will not tell.'

I was mortified. 'But why didn't you tell *me*? Why did you tell Esther and the others and not *me*. I thought we were friends . . . '

Gracie had never been a tactful person. She wasn't tactful now. 'Because we thought you might run and tell your mummy. Then they would have sent me home. And I would not be able to take my exams.'

I was so hurt, so wounded that they thought I would tell, that I was some kind of spy like Lovemore, that I forgot about Gracie's sufferings. I wanted to hurt her back.

'You only brought me here,' I raged at her, 'because you wanted to go with Levi without his mummy knowing!'

I regretted it as soon as I'd said it. But Gracie only shrugged. She didn't deny it. 'I love Levi,' she said simply. 'We are getting married very soon.'

'You must think I'm a complete idiot!' I yelled at her.

She didn't deny that either. I thought I was a fool too, for not knowing what was going on. For thinking I could be part of Grace's life when her mind was tormented in ways I couldn't even guess at.

'I want to go home. I want to go back to St Mark's right *now*.'

Grace looked up in surprise. There was real concern for me in her eyes. But at the same time, her mouth gave a tiny twitch of amusement, like you do when you see a little kid in a tantrum. I got wilder, more frantic. 'This is the most boring holiday ever! I'm sick of sitting round on chairs. I do nothing else but sit on bloody chairs. I will catch the bus back to town today!'

'You have missed the bus today, you will have to go tomorrow.'

'Then I'll go tomorrow!'

'It is Christmas Eve tomorrow.'

I had forgotten all about Christmas. I couldn't even remember what day of the week it was. Back at school my mum would be decorating the house with silver stars and cotton wool blobs of snow.

I felt so strange, so lonely and disconnected. Like an astronaut, whose life-line is broken and he's got nothing to cling to and he's drifting further and further out into deep space.

'I'm still going home tomorrow,' I insisted.

'OK,' said Gracie. 'If that is what you really want to do.'

TEN

That night, with the little sisters wriggling beside me in their bed like a nest of puppies, I dreamed about Christmas at St Mark's.

In my dream I staggered into the school chapel in the middle of Midnight Mass. Outside there was pitch blackness. A shrieking wind was hurling rocks about, tearing trees out by the roots like teeth. Torrential rain made the track into a blood-red torrent—the whole country was shaken by earthquakes and violent storms.

But inside the chapel it was quiet and still. I sank down on a grass mat.

Hurricane lamps spilled a golden glow over people's faces. There was Augustus our house boy, the disgraced Lovemore, Mr Chilolo cradling his baby daughter Stella, still alive even though she'd died in St Thomas's last year of the measles. There was Mum and Dad and all my friends from school and Gracie happy and smiling and even Celeste our white goat with her head back on.

And all the people were singing Christmas carols together. You couldn't hear the storm outside. Just our voices rising into the roof in harmony. And I was sobbing in my sleep because it was so peaceful and beautiful and innocent and I knew all the time that it wasn't really happening . . .

My eyelashes were still wet when I was prodded awake by Ezekiel's scaly finger.

'What's the matter?'

'Missy, you must hurry. The bus to town will go without you.'

If anyone else was up I didn't see them. The house

was grey and cold, not warmed up yet by the sun. I rushed to get ready, my stomach clenching at the thought of having to spend another day sitting on chairs, with all this dark confusion spinning in my head.

I forced myself not to think about the rape, about N'daka, Heston, or Levi. I filled my mind instead with Christmas at St Mark's—with silver stars and sparkle. I couldn't wait to get back there.

I told myself, 'Once you get back to St Mark's everything will be all right.'

I got dressed, stuffed things into my suitcase, left the little sisters sleeping. 'Come on, Ezekiel, let's go.'

I was pleased that no one was up to say goodbye. I didn't even want to see Gracie. Better to slip away into the dawn, as if these days at her village—and the awful truths that I had learned here—had never happened.

Being on the move was better, it made it easier not to think. Ezekiel was quick as a gecko. He was carrying my heavy suitcase on his head but it was still hard to keep up with him. Only minutes ago the sun had hit the main street but already it was blazing hot. I was soaked with sweat, pestered by tiny black flies. M'lindi looked down on us. She was still cool, mysterious, hidden by morning mist.

'Where are you going?' I asked Ezekiel, batting the flies away. But he didn't answer. Instead he veered off into the bush. I lost him. Then I saw my suitcase wobbling above the high grass and went panting after it.

'Wait, wait!' I grabbed his skinny arm. He peered at me, like an old tortoise. 'I thought the bus stop was outside the village, near the football field.'

'No, no, no. Today it stop in the next village. Does not stop here today.'

And he was off.

Tall grasses shook pollen on my head. Thorns raked

my bare legs as I crashed after him, desperate not to be left behind.

He was standing, waiting for me to catch up, on the edge of a deep canyon. There were empty oil drums lying around and the tracks of heavy machinery baked into the mud. It looked like some kind of construction project that had never happened. No machinery was there now, no people. It was abandoned.

There was a dizzy drop, down to a yellow river on the canyon floor. There were people down there, looking small and busy as cockroaches.

And crossing the canyon, from our side to the other, was a rusty pipe, wide enough—just—for someone to walk on.

Oh no, I thought. Oh no. He must be joking.

He wasn't.

Ezekiel, with a light and springy step, began walking over the pipeline, balancing my suitcase on his head, casually, as if he was strolling across a proper bridge.

'Wait, I can't get over there.'

He called back, 'You will miss the bus!'

I clambered onto the pipe, tried to stay upright like Ezekiel. I spread my arms like a tightrope walker, tottered a few steps, lurched forward, sickeningly—then collapsed to my knees, hugging the pipe, my face pressed against the hot metal and my head swimming. Someone high-stepped over me and with easy loping strides, *ran* along the pipe. If I didn't hurry Ezekiel would be gone and my suitcase with him. All my money was in there, my bus fare back to St Mark's.

Driven by panic, I began crawling after him, my legs and arms rubbery with terror, my breath sobbing.

I was thinking, Ezekiel's going to steal my money. As I inched along the pipe a voice gibbered inside my head. 'That old bastard. That sneaky old bastard!'

But Ezekiel was waiting for me at the other side.

'Why did you come this way?' I yelled at him, even before I'd reached safety. But my voice was lost in the great airy space below me.

I hauled myself the last few feet, slid off the pipe, staggered shakily over to him. 'I nearly fell off that pipe. Didn't you see? I nearly fell off!'

'Missy, this is the only way. The only way to reach the bus.'

A woman with a bundle of firewood on her head and a baby strapped to her back strolled across the pipe and disappeared into the high grass.

I snatched my suitcase off him. 'I'll carry that, if you don't mind.' I felt a sudden rush of shame as his gentle face creased in bewilderment.

He left me at the side of a wide dirt road.

'Bus will be here soon,' he said and ducked back into the bush.

I was completely alone. I had no idea where I was.

A man cycled past with a string bag of green gourds on the handlebars of his bike. He peeped at me sideways, cycled back to have a longer stare. Then went off again whistling.

M'lindi was clear of mist, bright emerald green and streaked with waterfalls like silver blood.

There was no shade. I waited and waited in the hot sun. What if the bus didn't turn up? I daren't let myself even think about it. I knew I couldn't go back across that pipe.

A woman joined me at the bus stop. I was pathetically relieved.

She had a crisp green and yellow dress on and a turban to match—the Party colours. She must be going off to a political rally somewhere. She had a proud, handsome face.

'Excuse me,' I asked her. 'Is there a bus to town today?'

'There is,' she said. 'It will be here soon.'

Then she didn't seem to notice me any more.

M'lindi was dazzling now. So bright she nearly blinded you. The sunshine struck her like a great golden gong. I wondered what time of day that made it. If you lived here, you could read her like a clock.

The bus came. When I saw that dust cloud in the distance I almost wept for joy. It was packed with people travelling for Christmas. I had to stand, crushed between the woman in the green and yellow dress and a man who talked non-stop about a deal he was doing on a second-hand Datsun.

'The next time I come this way,' he told everyone, 'I will be driving my own car. I'll give you a lift.'

Some people got off so I got a seat. I didn't think about Grace or my three days in her village. I fixed my mind on how amazed my parents would be to see me. 'What? You travelled all the way back to St Mark's on your own?' They would think I was so grown-up.

When I climbed down from the bus in the centre of town, lugging my suitcase, I was confused by the darkness, dazed by the lights in the shops. Last minute Christmas shoppers crowded the pavements. 'Rudolph the Red-Nosed Reindeer' came blaring out of the biggest, most brightly lit store.

'Hey!' I yelled, spinning round. Someone had banged into the back of my legs. It was a beggar. He trundled, on a little cart, out of an alleyway. He was pushing the cart along with two sticks, as if he was rowing a boat.

'Missy, give me shilling,' he said, holding up a leathery arm.

He had stumps where his legs should be and the skin on them was all puckered-up, like a drawstring bag. My money was in my suitcase. There was no way I was going to open it here, in front of these crowds, with all those sanitary towels inside.

'Shilling, Missy—'

I ran.

He chased after me. 'Shilling! Shilling!' He could row that little cart faster than I could run.

I dodged into a shop where he couldn't follow. He shot backwards, rowing his cart in reverse. I was safe.

'Missy, may I help you?'

The shop owner was breathing down my neck.

'No! No!'

I ran out, dragging my case, pushed my way through the crowds to the crossroads where there was the only set of traffic lights in town and the clock tower. All the time I was looking out for the metallic blue of my dad's VW, hoping against hope that he had come into town for something. He hadn't. But St Mark's was only six miles down the road and I was going to catch the last bus, the five o'clock bus to the turn-off.

It was seven o'clock. I couldn't believe it. All my arrangements fell to pieces. How had I got the time so wrong?

I stood gawping at the clock face. I asked some black-suited official hurrying home with a briefcase. No mistake, it was seven o'clock. The last bus was long gone.

I felt disorientated, panicky. As if the world was still running on its rails but I had somehow slipped clean off the track. I looked around for help. In all those swarming crowds there was no one I knew. It seemed as if there was a great, uncrossable distance between us. They seemed tiny and miles away, as if I was looking at them through the wrong end of a telescope.

I was on my own, scared and desperate. It was dark and much later than I thought. Soon the shops would shut and the centre of town would be empty. I made a really stupid decision.

I thought, I'll walk back to St Mark's. I'll be home for Midnight Mass in the school chapel.

All I had to do was follow the M1 to the turn-off. And not stray into the bush. The M1 was easy to follow. It was the only tarmacked road in the country.

I started walking, heaving the suitcase.

There were street lamps on Acacia Drive, the road I took to get out of town. There were no potholes in the road. It was an exclusive neighbourhood for ministers and top government officials. Sprinklers played all day to keep their lawns green. Rosebud lived somewhere round here. But I had no idea which was her house.

I saw no one. A car swung its headlights over me, then sped away. It was so quiet and deserted here that there could have been a curfew.

A curfew! That thought jolted me for a second. I looked round, half-expecting to see a lorry sneaking up on me, with its lights off, crammed with soldiers. Then I remembered the crowds of shoppers in town. 'Fool,' I told myself. 'It's Christmas Eve. There will be no curfew tonight.'

When Acacia Drive ended, there was blackness. In front of me was miles of bush. But I wasn't lost. The M1 glistened like black mercury in the moonlight, showing me the way home. There were no cars on it— even in the day there were hardly any cars. I got my torch out of my suitcase. Then I began walking down the highway.

'What's that?'

Something scuttled out of the way when I shone the torch into the bushes. I didn't do that again. I just moved into the middle of the M1. I walked slap bang down the middle of that highway as if it was a charmed path that would lead me safely through the wild wood.

And all the time I was thinking, When I get back to St Mark's everything will be all right. When I got back all this confusion in my head would clear. Things would get sorted out.

My torch went out. I shook it. It glimmered feebly, then went out again. I couldn't see the tarmac. I could only feel it, sticky, under my flip-flops.

Without my torch, every step in that whispering dark made me more and more twitchy. That suitcase was cracking my muscles. I opened it, got rid of all those horrible thick sanitary towels I'd been lugging around for so long. Good riddance, I thought as I hurled them into the bush.

Something whooped, the bushes crashed. I saw a flash of yellow eyes, they vanished. My heart was beating very fast.

There were drums in the distance—and a red fire glowing somewhere in the bush.

I stood shivering, in the middle of the empty M1. I was sure I wasn't alone. There seemed to be rustlings, sliding shapes all round me, as if there were people out there, circling me, closing in . . .

So when the car came along I waved my arms at it frantically. It blinded me with its headlights.

I yelled, 'Stop, please, stop.'

I thought it wasn't going to. But, at the last minute, it swerved over to the side of the road and waited, with the engine running.

I ran towards it. Everyone hitched on the M1. There weren't many cars or lorries. But those you saw were always jam-packed with people they'd picked up along the way. Even the army trucks gave people lifts.

I yanked the passenger door open, threw my suitcase (it was a whole lot lighter now) into the back. 'Thanks for stopping.'

'Well, I wasn't going to,' said the driver. 'Then I saw that you were white.'

I realized who it was. It was Father Ignatius.

That creepy man—I didn't like him. But I got in. I didn't have a choice. His 2CV might be the last car along this road tonight.

The rattling metal made my teeth throb as he bounced the little car out of the ruts back onto the M1.

I didn't think he would recognize me—but he did. 'You are from St Mark's. Right?' he said in his guttural voice. 'The one who cannot see the beauty of numbers?'

I thought, He's been drinking. When he turned towards me he breathed fruity alcohol fumes over me.

'And what are you doing out here on your own? It is not safe for a white girl to be out here.'

His face was flushed bright pink. His round gold-rimmed glasses glimmered in the dark. His white robes made him look ghostly.

The car drifted across the road. The headlights briefly showed a terrified face, then swept past it.

Father Ignatius wrestled with the wheel until the M1 shone straight and glassy in the headlight beams.

'Ach, these natives,' he said. 'Why do they always walk in the middle of the road?'

I hunched up in my canvas seat, keeping as far away from him as possible. I stared ahead through the windscreen into the night.

There was a pistachio-green mantis, one of the big leafy-looking ones, trapped by a wing under the windscreen wipers. Its legs were kicking feebly.

'I have been to the Gymkhana Club in the capital,' said Father Ignatius. 'Their *phiri-phiri* chicken is very good. Also their curry puffs. And we had wild strawberries for dessert.'

I knew about the Gymkhana Club. My mum and dad would not go there. It was full of white business people. The only black people were the waiters.

'I have had a good dinner with friends,' said Father Ignatius. 'And now I am on my way to the Lake. To

Zinja to spend Christmas at the mission school. Do you know that place?'

I murmured, 'Yes.'

He was very chatty. He seemed to have forgiven me for not loving numbers the way he did.

'I will have a very good Christmas dinner there,' said Father Ignatius. 'They pass the port round after dinner. They even had a Stilton cheese last time I was there.' Father Ignatius's eyes were bright and excited at the memory.

As we rattled along I half-listened to him talking about the good food he was going to eat. But mostly I thought about St Mark's. About getting back there just in time for Midnight Mass in the school chapel. And how I would creep in and stand at the back, just listening to the carols, before I joined in.

'We are almost at the turn-off,' said Father Ignatius. 'I will run you up to school.'

'No, no,' I started to say. 'There's no need. I know the way from here—'

Then I saw the chameleon. It was inside the car, sneaking with deliberate delicate movements up the Father's long skirts. Its eyes were swivelling wildly. And it was already bleaching itself ghostly white, to match his robe.

The girls at school were scared of chameleons. Chameleons meant the most terrible bad luck. They would never touch one. Esther said, 'They are witches in disguise. If you touch their skins you will die for certain. A woman in our village, she touched one and died.' I didn't touch chameleons either.

I tried to warn Father Ignatius.

'Father, there is a chameleon in your car, look, climbing up your clothes.'

He looked down, surprised, took a hand off the wheel and reached down.

'No, don't touch it. They're witches.'

'Ach,' he said, 'what superstitious rubbish! Only ignorant natives believe that. Now, how did that get in here?'

He tried to brush it off. But the chameleon gripped his hand with its tiny claws, like a baby clutching your finger.

I shrank away. But Father Ignatius tried to shake the chameleon off, out of the car window. It clung on. Father Ignatius shook his hand violently. The car swerved; he struggled to get control. We hit something.

The 2CV spun, light as a coin. It flipped over onto its side. I rattled about inside it. I cracked my skull on something metal. With a terrible grating sound, the car slid across the M1 . . .

I slumped there, tasting salty blood in my mouth. I didn't know whether I was right way up or upside-down. I didn't know how long I crouched in that canvas seat, dazed and dizzy. Maybe minutes, maybe hours. Then I became aware of someone groaning right beside my ear. Painfully, I turned my head.

Father Ignatius was sprawled next to me, his beautifully manicured hand clamped like a giant spider to his face. There was blood trickling in-between his fingers. He groaned again. He seemed to have hurt his head.

Then his body jerked, jerked again and he was awake. He began wrenching at the door in a frenzy, without noticing that I was sitting right beside him.

'Father Ignatius!'

He didn't even look round.

Frantically, he hurled his shoulder against the door. I watched him helplessly. I couldn't seem to move my arms or legs, my head ached. Someone was whimpering softly—it must have been me. Father Ignatius thudded into the door again and again, making the car rock.

Suddenly, the door shot open, he fell out, staggered to his feet and swooped off into the dark like a big white bat.

It was a few minutes more before I realized, for certain, that we had come off the road and crashed into a ditch.

'No good sitting here, Trish,' I told myself. But I still felt groggy, disconnected, as if I was trapped in a dream.

'Get out of the car,' I told myself.

My door was buckled up like a crumpled tin can. It wouldn't open. So I crawled across and got out the driver's side.

I sagged against the crushed bonnet, as if my leg bones were rubber. I didn't think of getting help. Once Father Ignatius had disappeared from the scene my brain forgot him, as if he'd never existed.

There was one clear purpose, shining like a star in my foggy brain. It was to get back to St Mark's for Midnight Mass.

I forced my body into shaky movement. At least I knew where I was. I was almost home. There was Mr Khan's shop where I bought my bras—the shop was dark, barred and shuttered. And just behind it was the huge swollen trunk of the baobab tree where Lovemore hid himself on St Mark's Day. The only light was from the moon and a glimmer from the bar beside Mr Khan's.

As I passed by the open door, a slurred voice invited me in, 'Come on, Missy. It is Christmas! Come and share a drink with us!'

I glanced that way. There was a man in a golden crown. 'I am king,' he told me. 'I am king just for one night!' He tipped his head back and roared with laughter.

I hurried away. I don't know how I found my way up the track to St Mark's without a torch. Halfway up I realized that I'd left my suitcase in the crashed 2CV. But that didn't seem to trouble me much.

'Pick it up another time,' my fuddled brain told me.

There was only one thing that mattered—getting home before the stroke of midnight. Like Cinderella, if I made it, then everything would be all right.

I didn't check for the mad golden eyes of stalking leopards or shudder at the whoops and sudden rustlings in the bush. I stumbled on through the perils of the night, as if I was protected by charms.

Can't wait to see their faces! The thought of how my parents would look when they saw me made me giggle hysterically. Once I'd started giggling, I didn't know how to stop.

But the school chapel, when I reached it, was locked. The windows were dark and cold.

I thought, What's going on here? I kicked at the side door as if they were deliberately locking me out.

I was angry and hurt, like a disappointed child. Hot tears stung my cheeks. When I smeared them away, there was blood on my hand.

I thought vaguely, I think my head's bleeding, but it didn't seem very important.

I went round to the main door, sure that it would be open to let me in.

As soon as I rounded the corner of the church strong lights dazzled me. I shielded my eyes, crouched back in the shadows. The school was lit up like a football stadium. Lights blazed from every classroom, from the boys' dormitories. Someone had switched the generator on after 9.30!

A prim voice in my head said, 'They shouldn't have done that. It's against the rules. Mum will give them a detention.'

Then I realized, in a dazed, unsurprised way, that the whole school was swarming with troops. They were in camouflage gear, like the *askari* we had seen at the swimming hole. But these were not comic book soldiers. Their rifles were real, they had real grenades slung across their chests. They crunched in columns along the neat gravel paths of the quadrangle. Their jeeps churned up the flower borders, mashing the lovely red Kaffir lilies. That was against the rules too.

I thought woozily, That will make my mum really angry. She will tell them all off.

There were barked orders, running men, gunfire. My head was aching more than ever—blue neon lights were flickering inside it. I felt suddenly very ill. Then I saw them drag someone out of a classroom. He was shuffling like an old man. That's because he was shackled hand and foot. They screamed at him, clubbed him down to his knees with a rifle butt. His school uniform shirt hung in tatters on his back.

When they hauled him up by the hair, I saw his wild terrified eyes, like a beast in the slaughter house. It was N'daka.

My shattered mind couldn't make any sense of it. I felt oddly detached, just an on-looker, as if I was at one of Mr Chilolo's boring open-air movie shows. It didn't hold my attention at all—the army take-over of St Mark's.

They slung N'daka into the back of a truck and hustled up other boys, also stumbling in chains. But I couldn't make out any more faces in all that shouting confusion. Trying to focus made me feel sick, made the blue lights in my head go berserk. So I just stopped watching, slid down onto the rough bricks of the porch floor, hugging myself tightly in my arms.

'When this is over,' I whispered to myself, 'it'll be time for Christmas.'

In the brilliant glare of the quadrangle, lit by headlamps from army jeeps, there was a lot of activity. Someone was squealing, on and on and on, like a baby pig . . .

Time passed. Perhaps I dozed off. When I woke the jeeps were going away, bumping up the track to the M1. The classroom lights stayed on but nothing moved in the pale, luminous square of the school compound. I huddled back into the church porch, waiting. But no one came to let me in for Midnight Mass.

ELEVEN

Two days later, when I felt better, I went down to the turn-off, to Mr Khan's, on an errand for my mum.

The king from the bar was in there, buying a packet of Daz, still wearing his battered golden crown. It was Francisco, our school clerk. I hadn't recognized him on Christmas Eve.

He said, 'Why did you not drink with us the other evening?'

He told me he had been playing one of the three kings in the hospital nativity play.

He said, 'I was the one who brought a gift of frankincense to the Baby Jesus.'

He asked me what kind of gift frankincense was but I said I didn't know.

Outside the bar someone was sitting drinking beer in a canvas chair. It was one of the seats from the crashed 2CV.

'It is a very bad thing about the school,' said Francisco.

'What will you do now?'

He shrugged, 'I will go to the city, stay with my brother, get a job there. It is too quiet here anyway. Nothing ever happens.'

The government was closing down St Mark's. The radio news said we were, 'A nest of sedition'. N'daka's father, it said, was plotting a coup. He had been arrested along with all his family. Except for N'daka, who had fled back to St Mark's and hidden out in the boys' dormitories with some of his cousins. But Lovemore's replacement had spotted them. He had told the authorities.

'Do you think N'daka was guilty of plotting against the government?' I asked Dad.

'N'daka? He couldn't plot his way out of a paper bag!' said Dad, with a bitterness in his voice that I'd never heard before. 'He wasn't capable of it.'

You don't know what he was capable of, I thought.

I didn't feel sorry for him, like Mum and Dad did. I wanted to tell them the truth: 'That N'daka, he was disgusting.' But I had to keep my mouth shut. I had sworn to keep Gracie's secret. I carried it with me, like Gracie's beads that I'd kept warm in my hand. Keeping quiet was the only service I could do her.

And it was even more important, now that all N'daka's family were being hunted down. What would happen to Heston if they found out that he was N'daka's son?

Mum and Dad couldn't understand why N'daka had tried to hide out at St Mark's. Even for someone whose head was as empty as a basket, it seemed a crazy thing to do. But I knew why. He believed, like I had believed, that St Mark's would protect him. That he would be safe here. That soldiers could prowl around outside but wouldn't get permission to come in.

We were lucky, Mum, Dad, and me. We weren't arrested. But we were caught up in the witch hunt. They gave us one week to leave the country. My parents were shattered. They couldn't believe it.

'It's so unfair,' said Mum. 'We were so careful. We always respected the law.'

We were alone on the hill top now. The day after the army closed down the school, Augustus didn't show up for work. He never came any more. The other staff slipped away. The generators were shut down and we had to pack all our things for UK by candlelight. Even our water supply, from up the bluff, was mysteriously cut off. Almost overnight sunflowers invaded the netball court.

113

I wandered through the eerie emptiness of the girls' dormitory, heard my friends' ghostly chatter in my head. Imagined Esther writing letters home on paper that she'd bartered for stolen coffee. Imagined Gracie looking like a princess in her blue and scarlet *zambia*, heard her laughing and joking. I heard her saying, '*Cha!* You are still a baby yet, aren't you?'

And I thought, No, I'm not Gracie. Not any more.

But I tried not to think about Gracie too much. It was too painful. I still missed her badly.

On one day, when Mum and Dad had driven to town to close their bank account, I climbed Lovemore's baobab tree and hid in its branches like he'd done. From my look-out post up there I could see the black shell of the burnt-out 2CV. People had stripped it, set it on fire. I'd seen a gang of kids setting off for the swimming hole with an inner tube from a car tyre to play with.

'That white man,' Francisco told me, when I met him buying Daz. 'That *azungu* from the car. He was in the hospital. They stitched up his head, many stitches. He was very angry—that he was missing his Christmas dinner at Zinja!'

I already knew that—what had happened to Father Ignatius. After my concussion had worn off, I'd made it up the hill and told my parents about the accident. But by now it was hours later. It was Christmas Day. They'd rushed down to the turn-off, expecting to find the Father's half-eaten body or just his bones. But there were no gory remains. He'd survived. Someone had found him staggering around and taken him to St Thomas's. Touching the chameleon didn't kill him after all. He was lucky.

I also knew what had happened to N'daka's father. It was on the radio that he had died suddenly, in prison, of pneumonia.

'Pneumonia!' scoffed my dad.

But even though they were being deported and even though there was no Young Pioneer Instructor sneaking round to spy on them, my parents wouldn't say outright what everyone believed—that N'daka's dad had been tortured to death in prison.

'Perhaps,' said my mum, 'he did die of pneumonia. After all, he was a very frail old man.'

There was no news on the radio about N'daka. None at all. He seemed to have vanished from the face of the earth.

When I got back from Mr Khan's shop, with the maize flour for my mum, I met Augustus. He was carrying off some of the cooking pots from the kitchen.

'So,' he said to me, 'you are still here then?'

He put down his stack of cooking pots and sat down on the *khonde* where he had served breakfast so often. I sat down beside him.

'What will you do,' I asked him, 'now that St Mark's is closed?' I just assumed he would be completely lost without St Mark's, like my parents were.

But he said cheerily, 'I will keep goats.'

I picked at the scab of a mosquito bite on my leg. 'How many goats have you got?'

'One, the white one your father gave me. And she is pregnant so I may have three, four goats!'

'You will be a rich man soon.'

The sky was pure blue, the light was good. You could see a long, long way today. I gazed out over the vast plain—the maize fields, tea plantations, the clusters of black huts. Right on the horizon—in a blurry pink haze, was a mountain . . .

'Augustus?' He was picking up his cooking pots ready to go.

'Ya, Missy?'

'Is that Mount M'lindi over there?' I pointed.

He squinted, shaded his eyes. 'Ya, Missy.'

'I never noticed it before.'

Augustus shrugged, 'When it is clear, you can see her.'

He went off, whistling, striding away with loose-limbed easy steps.

I sat on the *khonde*, looking at M'lindi. I wondered if Grace was looking at her too, at this exact same second. Whether she was with Levi and his mummy, or with Heston, or with her little sisters. I didn't suppose she would be thinking about me. Why should she?

I gazed down at my big, white flatfish feet. And thought about what Gracie must have suffered last term at St Mark's. Being able to see M'lindi from our dormitory, reminding her that the ones she loved best, Heston and Levi, were so far away. While N'daka, the one she hated most, swaggered about right under her nose, tormenting her.

And I didn't have a clue about any of it. Looking back, there were so many things I didn't understand— or that my friends couldn't tell me.

Finding that out was the most painful discovery of all.

TWELVE

Mum and Dad couldn't believe they had to leave. The last few days were a mad rush. Mum went round tight-lipped, ticking lists. They shipped things back to UK, packed other things for the flight, said goodbye to the doctors at St Thomas's. But all the time they never *really* believed it. They thought it was some kind of official mix-up.

Even at the last minute, when the taxi dropped us off at the airport in the city, they were peering anxiously round, hoping against hope that some government official would come running up, waving a piece of paper. 'Stop. There's been a terrible mistake. You have to stay. We need you!'

Of course, no one did.

And me? 'You must make a fresh start in UK,' I kept telling myself. I was pretty nervous about it—what those UK girls would think of me. But what else was there to do?

I didn't go into our dormitory, in those last few days. I looked in once, through the windows, and there were already ferns, pushing their way up through the shower room floor. When it was clear, I was careful not to look at the horizon. In case I saw M'lindi and started remembering.

But when we were waiting, on those sticky plastic seats in the airport, thoughts of that room in Levi's house sneaked into my mind. I couldn't help it. With the fan clunk-clunking overhead and the wailing music and Gracie's red beads in my hand.

'Surely,' said Dad, 'that can't be Grace? What's she doing here?'

My head shot up.

'And who is that baby on her back?' asked Mum.

I leapt up. 'That's her little brother, Heston!' I told her. I was already running to meet Gracie.

Gracie stepped across the airport lounge straight as a reed with that upturned chin, that regal look she had, like she was a princess. She had Heston slung on her back and she was carrying a string bag with some mangoes and sugarcane in it.

'*Cha!*' was the first thing Gracie said to me. 'I thought that I would miss you. Those buses, they are always late. And Heston, he is so heavy now.'

She untied Heston from her back and showed him to me. He didn't look pleased to see me. But at least he wasn't screaming his head off. He must have got used to *azungus*.

I almost daren't ask her. 'Did you come—I mean— are you here, *specially*?'

'What you think, girl? Think I have come all this way for nothing? Of course I came special. My bones are still aching from that bus ride! I have come to see you off. To wish you happy journey.'

I felt myself grinning like an idiot. 'You came all this way?'

'I said so!'

'*Ahhh.*' I didn't know what else to say.

'So!' said Gracie. 'You are really going to UK? You lucky girl. I would like to be in your boots.'

'No, you wouldn't,' I teased her. 'You would rather stay here with Levi and Heston.'

'Well, you are right,' she said, without even a hint of apology. 'I lied. I don't want to go to UK.'

I thought, Same old Gracie. I was so happy to see her. So proud of her. She lit up that dingy airport lounge like a brilliant blue and scarlet flower.

I didn't have much chance to speak to her privately.

Mum and Dad muscled in. They admired Heston. They asked her where she would take her exams, now that St Mark's was closed down. She said, cheerily, 'Oh, at a school near my home. I am very happy because I shall be able to see my boyfriend more often.'

And they looked a bit crestfallen, because St Mark's closing had not left the massive hole in her life that it had in ours.

But, just before our plane boarded, when Mum and Dad were fussing about with luggage and passports, there was a moment for some last words.

I said to Gracie, 'You won't see N'daka again. I think they have killed him.'

Her face became deadly serious: 'Ya, I think you are right. But Heston is still not safe.'

She gripped him closer as he wriggled about in her arms.

I nodded to show I understood. 'I'll keep your secret,' I promised her.

She smiled at me, a quick, sad smile. She stuck out her hand to shake mine. It was a strange, formal parting. But I wasn't disappointed. It was dignified somehow— the proper way to do things. And it helped me keep my feelings in check. Otherwise I might have made a fool of myself. I might have howled as loud as Heston did, that first time he saw me.

Gracie had turned to walk away.

I thought, with sudden, frightful panic, She's really going.

'I will write you letters, to your village!' I called frantically after her.

She startled me by turning back. '*Eeeee*,' she said, one hand flying to her mouth. 'I almost forgot.'

Swapping Heston into the crook of her left arm, she pulled a roll of bright yellow cloth out of her string bag and let it flap open, like a flag.

'What is it?'

'It is a gift from Esther. It is a tray cloth. See, she sewed it for you with her own hands. Here, take it.'

Gracie thrust the tray cloth at me. It had, 'TRISH! HAVE HAPPY DAYS IN UK!' sewn on it and all around the edge Esther had embroidered some big, clumsy blue flowers.

'Esther is not very good at sewing,' said Gracie, tactless as ever.

But I was touched, I really was. I had to swallow the lump in my throat before I could speak.

'What are those blue flowers?' I asked Grace.

'Ah! I forgot to say about those. Esther says they are these things called daffodils. They grow in UK. She copied them from a picture she found in an old magazine.'

'Was it a black and white picture?'

'Why?' asked Gracie, sharp as a pin.

'Because daffodils are supposed to be yellow,' I said before I could stop myself.

Grace threw back her head and laughed, a deep, throaty chuckle: 'That Esther. She is an uneducated girl. She doesn't know anything about UK. I will tell her. I will tell her those flowers that grow in UK are not blue!'

'No, you mustn't tell her that,' I begged Gracie.

'OK,' agreed Grace. 'I will not then.'

'Just tell her I like her present very much. I like her blue daffodils.'

My mum and dad were shouting at me. 'Hurry up!' It was the last call for our plane. There was no more time left.

'I am going now,' said Gracie.

'Bye, then. Thanks for coming—you know, to see me off.'

'*Cha!*' Gracie tossed her head as if it was nothing.

I gripped her arm. 'I'll come back, you know, Gracie.
I swear it. One day, I'll come back.'

'I will see you then, Trish,' said Gracie.

And she strolled out of the airport, with Heston on
her hip and the string bag of mangoes dangling casually
from her hand.

I could see nothing but white clouds from the plane
windows. We were not going far in this plane, only to
Nairobi, and then we would change into a big jet for
UK.

Mum and Dad were sitting behind me. They were
whispering to each other. I think Mum was crying, very
quietly, so she didn't disturb the other passengers.

I held Esther's tray cloth in my hand, with those
daffodils, defiantly blue. If anyone said to me in UK,
'Those must have been sewn by an uneducated person,'
I would step on the heel of their flip-flops.

In the pockets of my skirt there were some Kellogg's
cornflakes. I had stolen them from the kitchen, before
we left for the airport. I crunched them dry like we used
to do in our dormitory.

And in my head I held Gracie's secret. I would keep it
there for her. Until we met again. Just like I had kept
her beads, safe in my hand.